Margaret Barrington was born in 18[...]
three daughters of Richard Barringt[...]
Royal Irish Constabulary. Owing to [...]
early childhood was spent with her [...]
at Malin on the north coast of Do[...]
Dungannon Girls' School, Alexandra College, and Trinity College
Dublin, where she studied French and German. In 1922 she
married the historian, Edmund Curtis, but the marriage was
dissolved. She married the writer Liam O'Flaherty in 1926, from
whom she separated in 1932; there was one daughter, Pegeen,
born to them. During the 1930s she lived in London, where she
produced short stories for the BBC and edited the woman's page
for *Tribune*. A lifelong socialist and pacifist, she frequently offered
her services as an interpreter and translator for various left-
wing causes and supported the republican side in the Span-
ish Civil War. At the outbreak of the Second World War she
returned to Ireland, where she continued to write occasional
articles and short stories for *The Bell* and American newspapers.
She died in 1980.

My
Cousin Justin

Margaret Barrington

THE
BLACKSTAFF
PRESS

BELFAST

First published in 1939 by
Jonathan Cape Limited
This Blackstaff Press edition is a photolithographic facsimile
of the first edition printed by The Alden Press, Oxford

This edition published in 1990 by
The Blackstaff Press Limited
3 Galway Park, Dundonald, Belfast BT16 0AN, Northern Ireland
with the assistance of
The Arts Council of Northern Ireland

Printed by The Guernsey Press Company Limited

British Library Cataloguing in Publication Data
Barrington, Margaret 1896–1980
My cousin Justin. I. Title
823.912 [F]
ISBN 0-85640–456–X

PART I

MY COUSIN JUSTIN

NORTH the land lies in great tongues out into the sea, protected by walls of black basalt, heavy, rounded, smooth as a belly. Where these bens do not present an even front to the ocean, the sea pours in over rocks and sand-bars, forming long, sandy bays which lie golden and blue under the summer sun, bleak and wind-swept in the winter storms.

At the foot of one of these little bays, sheltered by green hills, lay the village of Glasthule. Beyond the hills stretched the great moors rising gradually to the heights of the Slieve Dhu range. It lay cosy and snug, like an egg in the nest, forty houses or so, squat, whitewashed dwellings, golden-thatched, the roofs fastened with ropes and weighed down with stones. They surrounded a triangular green on which geese of unknown age and ownership grazed. The veterans of the troop waddled slowly across the green, trailing their heavy dewlaps, turning their heads gracefully as they picked daintily here and there, and pecking savagely at the youngsters, did they dare to advance in front of their elders — a well-disciplined body.

At the south corner of the green, near the church, there stood, apart from the other houses, a grey stone building. It was built in the French style, round a cobbled courtyard, and showed a bare front and dark shuttered windows to the world. On two sides of this courtyard lay the house proper, shaped like the letter L, on the third side the barns, and facing the road a wall some twelve feet high with strong wooden gates. Beside the gates were two high stone mounting-blocks and along the wall were set iron rings to which horses could be tied. Beyond the barns lay the backyard, the stables, the byres and hen-houses, and beyond that again the gardens, sloping up towards the green foot-hills, all surrounded by high stone walls. These walls were a shelter against the storms that swept across these parts, tearing trees up by the roots, and sweeping the roofs from the houses. But they also acted as a barrier, separating those within from those without. The house was like a fortified castle, keeping all at bay.

Here in this house lived my grandfather, John Thorauld. There fifty years previously he had brought my grandmother when they were both little more than boy and girl. Here their children had been born and reared in the old Huguenot tradition. From here they had scattered all over the world.

The house had been built some two hundred years ago by one of the Thoraulds, as a sort of country house or shooting lodge. It was strange that it should be built so far away from the old home, which lay in the rich lands of the Lagan, some thirty miles distant, peaceful, undisturbed by storms and winds, close to the spinning-mills which made the family fortune. There on the banks of the Suil

River the mill still stands, a high building, and beside it a smaller one on which is painted in black letters:

JEAN-JUSTIN THORAULD ET FILS

At the time of his marriage my grandfather had left this pleasant home and had never since gone back. Twice a year he received a letter from his nephew, a childless, middle-aged man whom we had never met. Twice a year he sharpened a goose-quill and replied.

It was here in this northern fastness, cared for by our aunt and grandfather, that my cousin Justin and I grew up, forgotten, it seemed, and abandoned by our families.

As I remember my cousin Justin, he was a tall, lanky boy, with long arms and legs. His pale face was covered with freckles, like a turkey's egg. His black hair grew off his forehead in a cow's lick and then fell over one eye. From under straight black brows, his dark eyes looked round in serious wonder. He rarely smiled.

In winter he wore a dark blue jersey, a reefer jacket with brass buttons and long blue sailor trousers. In summer the jersey was changed for a blue linen shirt. His clothes were made by the local tailor who insisted on making the bell-bottomed trousers, in true sailor fashion, to button up the sides. Justin detested them because the village boys jeered at them. But no matter how much he complained or implored, John Gallagher would not cut them in any other way. My own clothes were the same as his except that I wore a navy blue kilt. My reefer jacket was, as often as not, one of Justin's old ones.

He had a habit of standing, his legs wide apart, his clenched fist on his chest. He would never let anyone approach too near him, throwing out a warning hand to ward off the oncomer. He lisped slightly.

Within, the house was like a rabbit-warren, long passages with sudden dark corners and recesses. Like all Irish country houses, it smelled of oil lamps, peat smoke and apples. The rooms, strangely shaped and for the most part small, were unexpectedly warm and sunny. No two of them were alike. The furniture was gathered from all ages and arranged without regard to period or art. The walls were hung with portraits and daguerreotypes of various members of the family and of my grandmother's family, stern men soberly dressed in the fashion of their day, and here and there a frail but equally stern woman, with long resigned countenance and folded hands. Upstairs there was a multitude of examples of their handicraft, old samplers in the stiff French they learned to speak, tapestry pictures of sacred subjects, woolwork cushions, chair-covers and patchwork quilts. Their names lived in their work long after they were forgotten. These names, strange foreign names, handed down punctiliously for over three hundred years, were like those flowers which gleam, preserved yet dead, in the corners of old-fashioned drawing-rooms.

In winter, when for weeks heavy storms raged and doors and windows were fastened tight against the wind, we could hear the hammering of the waves on the bar. I used to dread the moment when I would have to take my candle and go along the dark passages to bed. Seated beside my cousin Justin on the settle in the kitchen, my bowl of porridge and cream on my knee, listening to Bella and Theresa joke with Wattie or with some neighbour who had dropped in to see them, I could not get my mind away from it. My constant terror was that the bar might break and the sea come tearing down the village to drown us all. I could see myself caught in the winding corridors as in a trap, unable to get out into the open where I could flee to the mountains. I often repeated to myself the lines of the psalm 'I will lift mine eyes unto the hills from whence cometh mine aid'. It is the only psalm I remember to this day.

Justin scoffed at my fears.

'Don't be such a silly ass, Loulie,' he'd say. 'The bar can't break. It will last until the day of Judgment.'

I didn't believe him. I felt in my bones that this was mere male bravado. Aunt Molly was more reassuring. After a rain-storm she pointed to a rainbow hung in the sky and said:

'See, Loulie, the dear Lord has placed the rainbow there as a sign and token to men that he would never again drown the world. We must trust Him.'

But my trust in divine Providence did not last long. When the next storm came I had decided that owing to the incurable wickedness of mankind, stressed on Sunday by grandfather, God would be perfectly justified in going back on his word. So my terrors would return, never to vanish completely.

In summer when the days were long and the nights full of light and the only sounds which reached my ears were pleasant domestic noises, these fears would recede. But the long winding corridors still held ghostly fears for me and I never traversed them without a quickening of the heart-beat, my ears sharpened for untoward sounds. As we pattered up to bed I would keep my weather eye open to be sure that my cousin Justin was close beside me.

Every evening Aunt Molly would call us in from yard or garden where we were playing and conduct us up to bed. In winter we each carried a brass candlestick which we took from a small table in the hall where they stood ready, and the procession wound its way upstairs, Justin and I close together, Aunt Molly and Bella following with the hot towels. In summer the long northern twilight lit up dimly the winding passages which led to our rooms. Bella had already prepared the bath. We had the same one and took turns at getting in first. Then, dressed in our night-gowns, we would say our prayers at Aunt

Molly's knee. The words of our prayers never varied except when someone was ill and we had to pray for his recovery. First we asked God to make us good children and keep us safe, then we asked Him to bless our parents whom we scarcely knew and did not want to know, for to us Aunt Molly and grand-father were sufficient. We asked Him to look after our various animals. Then together we recited the Lord's Prayer and jumped into bed. Aunt Molly tucked us up and told us to sleep well. She looked so sweet as she bent over us, her curly hair brushing our cheeks and her flowered skirts swinging against the valance of the bed. Aunt Molly gave us all the love we needed.

My cousin Justin slept in the great four-poster bed in the blue spare room and I in the dressing-room off it. Aunt Molly left the connecting door open so that we could talk. But when she had closed the outer door and her steps had grown fainter as she went down the passage, I would seize my pillow and go into the spare room. There Justin would be sitting up in bed, like a small island in a great sea.

'Move over,' I'd say, 'and give me my half.'

Then our adventures would begin. Each night we would set out on a journey round the world and visit some different country or have some strange adventure.

'Where shall we go to-night?' said Justin.

'The North Pole.'

'No, that's only nice in very hot weather.'

'Sweden then. Aunt Anne says the Swedes are the most polite persons in the whole world.'

'Maybe. But I think I'd rather go to a hot country to-night.'

'Java,' I suggested. I had been born in Java, though I remembered nothing about it.

'You're always wanting to go to Java. Let's go to India.'

'Where shall we go in India?'

'To the native parts, where there are no white men, where we shall be the only ones. Then everyone will have a great respect for us and give us things.'

'What sort of things?'

'Oh, you know. First of all a palace to live in, a beautiful white palace made of marble with beautiful gardens and stables full of horses and cows and elephants.'

'We shall go hunting,' I continued. 'We'll sit in chairs on an elephant's back and shoot tigers.'

'No, not shoot them,' cried Justin angrily. 'We'll catch them and bring them home with us.'

'But tigers are wicked. They eat people.'

'Even if they do, I'll tame them. They'll get quite fond of me when they see that I wouldn't hurt them.'

'What else shall we do?'

'We'll catch a couple of monkeys and bring them home with us. They can live in the palace too. They're never wicked.'

'Will they have babies?'

'Of course,' said Justin. 'Lots of babies. The house will be full of monkeys. And if anyone is particularly nice to us, or does something very noble, we'll give him a monkey. No one will have monkeys but us, and we will only give them to nice people who will be kind to them. You can have a monkey of your own if you like.'

'I don't think so. I'd rather just share yours.'

'All right. You can feed them sometimes. We shall have to grow a lot of monkey nuts for them, and of course bananas.'

'I like bananas.'

'You can have some of the bananas. Then when we are frightfully rich we'll come home here and bring the monkeys with us. We'll be famous because no one will have as many monkeys as we'll have. We'll build them a special house in the garden and have them to live with us in turns. They'll go on having babies and people will come and want to buy them. But we'll only sell them to very nice people and only for a lot of money.'

I was getting sleepy.

'What shall we do with the tigers when we leave? Give them to a zoo?'

'No, certainly not. We'll turn them wild again.'

'Even if they eat people?'

'Even if they eat people.'

In the morning after breakfast we had lessons with grandfather in the dining-room. He sat at the head of the table and wrote with a goose quill, which he cut himself from a goose feather. The geese in the yard seemed to be reared simply to provide grandfather with pens. He held the pen between his first and second finger, but when we tried to imitate him, he corrected us. He did not like to admit that he held it in this way because he was old and his hand was stiff.

Grandfather was a tall, rather stout man with a long white beard, rather like the picture of Moses that hung over the mantelpiece in Justin's room. But Moses in the picture was angry. He held the Tables of the Law high over his head and was just going to hurl them down to the ground because the Children of Israel, rather indistinct in the background, were worshipping a golden calf. All this had been done in wools by some lady of the family and had been carefully preserved as a memorial of her piety and good needlework. Yet grandfather was very like Moses and I think that it was this resemblance that kept us quiet and dutiful under his eye.

Justin learned Latin and Greek. We both learned arithmetic and a little algebra. I struggled to learn to write a neat hand, an achievement I never acquired. We read some history and learned French. We translated *Télémaque* and conjugated irregular verbs and learned to converse in stiff eighteenth-century phrases. Then grandfather, on watch for the first sign of boredom, would say:

'Enough for to-day. Blot your copybooks and run out.'

We were very fond of grandfather though he was more aloof than Aunt Molly. He never spoke to us as older people often do to children. He used to ask us to go to the village shop and buy his tobacco. We were always given a penny each for this errand. Grandfather smoked a particularly strong brand of plug, such as you can only find in country villages and sailors' stores. His room stank of it but it was impossible to cure him of the habit. He kept six pipes in a rack and smoked each in turn. He once described to us the terrible effects of having to give up tobacco. When once to please grandmother he had tried to stop smoking he had nearly died. The doctor ordered him to go back to his pipe and all was well. Grandmother never asked him to do such a thing again.

Every day he drank a bottle of whisky. He was constantly complaining of the price. When he was a young man, he used to declare, whisky was a reasonable price. Almost no duty had to be paid to an interfering government. It seemed to have little or no effect on him. On rare occasions, however, he would close himself in the 'office' and then we knew what was happening. Grandfather was getting drunk. Presently he would emerge in a towering rage. Terrified, we would cower in the kitchen where Bella would laugh at us and comfort us at the same time. Grandfather raged around the house and poor Aunt Molly would try in vain to pacify him. He used to curse the government which he declared had been the cause of his ruin. I have never since liked any government. Then he would tell Aunt Molly in stern tones that she would have to alter our way of living, if she did not want to be left destitute when he died. We would have to sell the horses and the house and go to live in a cottage. God damn her, what did she mean by spending so much money? What did she do with it? Look at those bills!

These outbursts always occurred around quarter day. By and by grandfather would get quieter and sit down by the fire muttering. Then Aunt Molly would come and herd us off to bed. Fond as we were of grandfather we were very frightened and lay shivering together in the big four-poster bed, praying hard to God to make grandfather sober again. Everything was just as usual the next morning. Grandfather paid the bills and all would go well until next quarter day.

After lessons we always ran out to the yard to visit our animals. Sometimes Wattie would saddle the ponies and we would go for a ride, through the fields or up towards the hills. Wattie was the yard-man, gardener and coachman. He smelled like grandfather, only worse. We did not like Wattie very much. He was always getting drunk and making scenes. When he drank too much, which he frequently did, he thought it his duty to tell the whole village what he thought of it. He made all sorts of reflections which the village took in good part because he was drunk but which would not have been tolerated for a moment had he been sober. All would go well indeed until he arrived at John Gallagher's cottage. The tailor was a man of hasty temper and he did not see eye to eye with Wattie politically. He would put aside the coat he was stitching and go out into the street. There would be words and then blows. Then someone would fetch grandfather. He would order Wattie home and then dismiss him. Next morning Wattie would go to the priest and take the pledge and then turn up at the house with it in his hand. He would be reinstated until the next time.

Indoors Bella was absolute monarch. A stout woman, dressed in the tight peasant bodice and a multitude of petticoats, over which she tied a stiffly starched apron, she wielded her potstick as Marshal Ney wielded his baton. Justin and I used to delight in teasing her by picking up her skirts from behind and slipping underneath. She would utter an unexpectedly feminine scream and whip round with that agility which is often so surprising in fat women.

'Take that, you young rip,' she would shout as

she brought the potstick down on the buttocks of the offender with the precision of a drummer.

No one ever entered the kitchen without receiving either a warning or a reprimand. No sooner was your hand on the latch than her voice boomed out:

'Mind and wipe your feet on the mat. I won't have ye sheddin' yer clabber all over my clean kitchen.'

Her conversation was shrewd and racy. She could curse fluently, so she boasted, in four languages — in the English, the Gaelic of Donegal, the Gaelic of Rachery, and the Gaelic of the Isles.

On the occasions when Wattie, as she put it, 'made a holy show of himself', Bella always took him in hand. If he were past reason or scorn, she would hoist him on the broad of her back like a sack of oats and bear him out to the stables where she bedded him in the straw and left him until such time as he sobered up. On re-entering the kitchen she would wash her hands with a Pilate-like gesture and smooth her black hair behind her ears with her damp palms. Then, patting herself all over, she would remark to Theresa who sat warming her shins at the fire:

'What can ye expect from a pig but a grunt.'

She treated Wattie with the contempt she felt for all men, pouring forth her scorn at every opportunity and accusing him of all manner of misdemeanours. He paid no more heed to her nagging than a duck does to water. He accepted the position of unofficial husband with equanimity. Every Saturday morning she would rout him out of bed at five o'clock to whitewash the kitchen. When he had finished she would stand looking at it and remark:

'Lord of Creation! Isn't it a queer thing but no man alive can do anything without making a dirt? Look at the floor, will ye? By rights I should make ye go down on yer marrow bones and scrub it. Heth! Since ever the curse of Adam fell on us, a man's no more use than a bull calf. What he does he has til be driven to, and when that's done, a woman must needs run after him, reddin' up.'

The only man to whom she rendered lip-service was grandfather. Sometimes he would ask her into his sitting-room, give her a glass of wine and ask her to sing some old Irish song while he accompanied her on the flute. Coming as he did from the Lagan, he would discover in her singing some strange phrase he had not hitherto heard. Seated on a stiff-backed chair, her skirts outspread, her hands folded on her lap, she sang the traditional melodies with an ever-fresh abandon. Then to please grandfather she would end by singing 'The Lark in Clear Air' in a voice as true and clear as that of the lark itself.

It was only when he attempted to intrude into what she considered her business that he met with an unconquerable obstinacy. On one occasion he produced his mother's cookery book and asked her to cook a dish of tripe in a special way. Bella listened with respect while he read out the instructions, then, with the aloof dignity of one asserting her rightful place in creation, she replied:

'It's not in nature to cook tripe without onions and milk.'

For dinner she served up tripe and onions cooked as she always cooked it. She placed the dish on the table with the air of saying: 'That'll learn ye.'

The only human being to whom she was unfailingly kind was our poor crazy Theresa. To Bella, Theresa was one of those 'afflicted by God' and as such must be given every care and consideration. She would say to Aunt Molly when Theresa, taken with one of her periodic fits of madness, had run away:

'She's one of God's creatures. Even the brute beasts know it. Look at the way the cows give their milk when she sings til them.'

Indeed it was a lovely sight to see Theresa milk. Her head nestled against the cow's gentle flank, her shrill voice rising in the old song — the pretty girl milking the cow — a lighthearted song of courtship and the only one the poor girl knew, she drew the milk in two long silken threads from the cow's udder.

Bella was very devout. It was a great grief to her that as heretics we were foredamned to eternal punishment. She grieved especially over me, Justin as a potential man could scarcely be counted in the scheme of creation. Quietly in the evening she would draw me to her side and teach me a Catholic hymn. I wish now she had taught me the songs she sang grandfather. She was in great demand at funerals. No one could raise the *caion* over the dead as she could.

Justin had a passion for collecting suffering animals. He preferred them to healthy ones. The loft was always full of them and I knew he hated them to get well, for then most of them would fly or run away. There were birds with broken wings and legs, a hedgehog he had rescued from a dog, a three-legged cat for which he made a small wooden leg so that for years it hopped around the house to Bella's great discomfort. She hated to hear the tap, tap of the little wooden splint during the night.

'It's no manner of use til no one,' she'd say. 'It can't catch mice and what's a cat good for but to catch mice?'

'It doesn't catch mice just to please us,' Justin replied.

'Well, that's what God made it for and without its four legs it's no kind of good and would be better off dead.'

But the cat lived on in spite of her and died of old age. He even became very expert at dodging the potstick which Bella in her culinary frenzies used sometimes to throw at him. But even Justin could not claim that he ever caught a mouse.

One day Aunt Molly said to us at breakfast:

'Now, children, it is Aunt Anne's birthday. Don't you think you could gather some roses in the garden and bring them to her? Grandfather and I will come along later.'

'What age is she?' asked Justin.

'Ninety-one, I think,' said grandfather.

'My goodness,' I said. 'Won't she die soon?'

'I don't think so,' grandfather replied smiling. 'She'll probably live for ever.'

'Or go up to heaven in a chariot of fire,' said Justin. 'That's what I want to do. I don't want to die, do you, grandfather?'

'I shan't mind very much,' he replied smiling.

'Now, run along, children,' said Aunt Molly, 'and don't forget the flowers.'

Aunt Anne was grandfather's stepsister, who lived in a small house just outside the village. She seemed to have spent most of her life roaming over the face of the earth and was very scornful of her present humble surroundings. Seated on a high-backed wooden chair, as stiff and as erect as a grenadier, she would look around her and wave her hand at the four walls of the little room in which she was sitting and say:

'And to think that I have sat down to eat with princes!'

We were always very impressed with this statement. That some of them were Indian princes added to the romance. Her white hair was piled high on her head and covered with black lace. She wore a wide-skirted grey dress, a white lace apron, a small white shawl round her shoulders and a coloured Indian necklace round her neck. She took snuff with an air of distinction, brushing off the grains that fell on her dress with a small lace handkerchief.

We arrived at her cottage with the roses. She received us graciously, just as if we were visiting royalty. We sat down on two stools opposite her on the other side of the fireplace. She gave us small glasses of sweet wine and slices of seed cake. Then she sat down again and looked at us.

'What age are you now?'

She asked us this question each time we visited her. She never seemed to remember. We supposed that she found our ages very insignificant compared with her own.

We told her.

'Dear me,' she remarked. 'You are growing up. Very tall children for your age. You take after our side of the family, both of you. You look very like your grandfather when he was a boy.'

We were, of course, very pleased to hear this, though we found it difficult to see where the resemblance came in.

'Tell me, Aunt Anne,' asked Justin, 'are tigers very fierce? Would they eat you if you were kind to them?'

'Certainly they would eat you,' she replied. 'Of course many of the native princes in India keep a

28

tiger cub as a pet, but they are very careful, and if he shows signs of becoming wicked they kill him.'

'How cruel!' said Justin.

'Not at all, the tiger would eat you without thinking anything about it.'

'Tell us about India, Aunt Anne,' I asked.

Aunt Anne was just about to launch into one of her interminable stories about the glories of the East or the horrors of the Mutiny when grandfather and Aunt Molly arrived. Aunt Molly was carrying a cake and grandfather brought a bottle of wine and a set of old chessmen.

'Happy birthday,' they said and kissed her.

'Happy birthday,' we echoed.

Grand-aunt became slightly tearful.

'Ninety-one. A long life. A very long time to have lived. Who would have thought that I would end it here, in this place? I, who have lived in so many places. I, who have enjoyed the company of the greatest in almost every country of the world.'

Grandfather laughed gently.

'You always remind me, Anne,' he said, 'of old sherry, well travelled.'

Aunt Anne tossed her head lightly.

'And what of it? It's a good thing to have pleasant memories when you are old.'

'You're not so old,' said Aunt Molly. 'Please God, you'll be spared to us for many a day.'

'You're as light on your feet as a young girl,' said grandfather. 'I'll take a bet with anyone that you can still dance a two-handed reel with the best of them.'

So the floor was cleared and Aunt Molly opened the old piano which stood in the corner of the room. Grand-aunt Anne took her place opposite grandfather and curtsied. Down to the ground she curtsied. Then the dance began. I have never seen such dancing. Their feet twinkled so fast that it was impossible to watch the steps. Round and round they went. Aunt Anne swayed to the music like a young girl, pirouetted on her toes like a ballet dancer, swung with agile step, her whole body alive with the rhythm of the music. Grandfather was the first to stop.

'You see, Anne, you can still dance everyone off the floor.'

We all sat down and drank some wine. Grandaunt's pale face was slightly flushed by the exercise but otherwise she seemed not in the least ruffled. Not a hair was out of place. She took a pinch of snuff and looked around in triumph.

'You are too fond of the pleasures of the table, John,' she said to grandfather.

Grandfather laughed.

'Happy days!' he said, lifting his glass.

We all drank.

JUSTIN waged an unceasing war with the boys of the village. This fight did not include the girls who were gentle creatures, living under the shadows of their mothers and occupied with small domestic tasks, such as minding the younger children or helping to bring in water and turf from the yard. They rather liked him because of his quiet manners. But the boys hated him because I think of his aversion from any familiarity and his contemptuous manner of addressing strangers. He loathed them because of their naive cruelty, which he could not understand, and which always drove him into fits of angry passion. Again and again he got himself badly beaten, and frequently brought the same punishment on my head by his wanton interference with their fun. He did not see why they should take any pleasure in tormenting an old donkey, in making dogs fight and in going ratting when the stacks were lifted. He could never control himself when he saw an animal teased or hurt. Also he was abnormally sensitive to ridicule. When we passed through the village on our way to the sand dunes, they would shout after us from some safe shelter, jeering at us both.

When summer was at its height and the sun blazed hot even in north Donegal, Justin and I would prepare for our descent on the village. This was the season of marble-playing when the weather was too close for more active games. It is a dull game, played singly or even in twos. It was a game, moreover, at which I excelled and consequently Justin would be left after a short time with no marbles in his bag. So, prepared to exploit my skill, he would gather all our marbles together, divide them equally between the two of us, though by rights most of them belonged to me, and we would set off for the village.

During the holidays the boys still hung around the school playground. Justin and I would wander around at some distance until they had begun a game. Then we would approach and spill our marbles out on the ground and ask if we could join in. The sight of our beautifully coloured glass balls, the larger ones costing as much as threepence at the village shop, some coming from far-off Derry, was irresistible. We would be allowed to play. There were generally about ten boys there. By rushing out of the house immediately after breakfast before their wary mothers had contrived to catch them and set them to some task, they could manage to have a free day. I was always the only girl present.

Generally Justin would lose one or two of the coveted glass marbles. He played no better and no worse than the others. I would watch Willie Quigley or Jim MacLaughlin rub them on his trouser leg and slip them into his pocket. In the end they would return to my bag. The play would go on for I was never invited to take part. After a while Justin would step back and say:

'Your turn, Loulie.'

No one as yet dared to object. I squared myself for the task. By the rules of the game you kept on until you missed. Then you placed a marble down and stepped back to await your turn. I had two methods of shooting. Sometimes, squatting on my hunkers, I would send the marble spinning along the ground in the orthodox way, but when I grew elated and wished to show off my skill, I would sit up and, taking aim, let the marble fly some twelve inches from the ground. This often smashed the marble it hit in two. So long as there was a marble left, it must be put down. Gradually the small group of boys would become silent, their young foreheads drawn into frowns. Justin would stand, his legs apart, just as if I were his dog and he were showing me off. We knew, however, how it would end. When I had pocketed the last marble, there would be a circle around me, not of admiring youths, but of furious beaten boys. They knew that we could always get more marbles and they could not. They might be forced to eke out the season with the cheap clay taws which were sold at the village shop for four a penny.

The fight always began slowly. Justin and I stood back to back, waiting. Their small hard fists held up, they came on. They never demanded their marbles back. They just punished us for our selfish-

33

ness. And it was punishment. Not one of them but could hit hard and place his blows well. I fought as girls do with nails and feet, but it did me little good. Surely we were driven out with bleeding faces and sore bodies. On one occasion I was set in flight by Egan O'Doherty who adopted the simple plan of making water on me. For years I remembered the incident with deep resentment.

At the end of grandfather's garden grew two yew trees, tall, dark gloomy trees, and between them there was a door which creaked open on rusty hinges. Beyond there was a little wood, an unusual thing in this country where few trees grew, for the north-west wind which blew almost all the year stunted and destroyed young trees. Even the hardy thorn bushes with roots twisted in the stony soil looked like ragged banners blown by the wind. But here it was sheltered and behind high walls a little wood had been planted. Through the middle of the wood, which we called Paradise, flowed a river. Before the river reached the wood it was a turbulent mountain stream, tumbling over naked boulders. But here it flowed slowly with scarcely any noise. Justin and I used to spend long hours here, imagining that it was indeed the garden of Eden. Flowers jewelled the thick carpet of mossy grass and in the spring great masses of kingcups spread along the bank. We used to lie on the edge of the stream or lean over the wooden bridge that spanned it and watch the fish, great lazy trout, lying there, head to stream, waiting for food. In the summer evening they would leap and jump out of the water, but in the heat of the day they would just lie there, letting the water pass through their gills, gently waving their tails to keep themselves steady in the water. We used to try to tickle them but we were not patient enough to become proficient in this art. The fish would give its tail an extra twist and away it would shoot through the water, so fast that the eye could not follow it. Wattie brought down some old fishing rods from the barn, made us some flies and taught us to throw a cast. But the first time Justin landed a fish he turned white, and tearing the hook out of its jaws he hurled it back again into the water and would never fish again.

We liked to wander through the wood, following the stream up to the mill, a high grey stone building with a water wheel. It was a sinister place. Many of the windows were broken and strange birds haunted it. The great heron would rise as we came near, flapping his leathern wings as he passed over our heads. When the mill was working there was a great noise of rushing water and the rattle of machinery. What made it more strange was that it was a house without a chimney.

In the mill we would find old Manus, the miller. He was an old man with thick white hair and a black beard lightly speckled with grey. He was still strong and active and prided himself on being able to carry heavy sacks of corn up to the top of the mill.

35

But he seldom did so now except when he wanted to boast of his strength. He was also a fiddler and story-teller, in great demand at dances and weddings. During the intervals between the dances, when the perspiring couples were resting, he told his stories. They were ages old, these stories, coming to him from his father and grandfather, for the profession of story-teller is for the most part hereditary. But he never told a story twice the same; he would alter it or add something different, something out of his own life or the life of someone present, or even something he had read in the paper. This was all part of the tradition.

He always looked up with a start when we stood beside him, for years of working in the mill had made him a trifle deaf. He would never admit that it might be old age coming on him. He would look at me, smiling and stroking his bushy black beard. Then the compliments would begin:

'You're growing to be a big girl, Miss Honeyball. It'll be no time at all until ye'll be flauntin' long skirts and givin' poor old Manus the go-by.'

Such talk always embarrassed me.

'Don't be silly,' I'd reply.

'As for you, young master,' he always addressed Justin with great mock respect. 'Time's comin' when ye'll be bigger and stronger than John L. Sullivan himself and he the strongest man in the world. Or maybe ye'll be a great sodjer like the famous Duke of Wellington.'

'I'll never be a soldier,' Justin would say angrily. Manus knew quite well why we had come over.

'Now, let's see,' he'd say. 'When last did we take your weights and heights? Come along to the scales.'

We'd be weighed and measured and the results written up beside the last ones on the back of the door. I always felt a slight grievance that I would never be so tall as Justin. He had the start of me and he was a boy. Then we would ask Manus to show us the mill. We never wearied of it. I think we could have seen the mill every day.

We would go up the rickety stairs to the very top where the corn was put in. I would stand and watch as sack after sack of oats was emptied into the great vat and then see it emerge at the other side all husked and good to eat. I loved to run my hands through it and take out a handful of kernels. Manus would hold me up so that I could look into the depths.

'Am I safe, Manus?' I would ask, holding tight to the collar of his coat.

'As safe as in God's pocket,' he would answer.

Then we went down the four floors of the mill, watching the corn as it was ground finer. Manus would never explain the process. Perhaps he did not understand it very well himself. But he loved making a mystery of it, pretending that only he and God knew anything about it. I always insisted that grandfather did. Manus would laugh and retort:

'Sure, how could he, Miss Honeyball? He's a gentleman and knows nothing about work. Else why should he get me to work his mill?'

We refused to listen to such treason.

'Grandfather knows everything.'

Sometimes Manus would tell us a story. He told us many stories, tales of Fion Mac Uail and the Red Branch, fairy tales and ghost stories. But none of them have stayed in my mind, perhaps because they changed so much with each telling. But afterwards when I read old legends I would find that I already knew part or all of them and I am sure I heard them from Manus. He would sit on a pile of sacks with us opposite him. He made a great ceremony of the beginning, cutting the plug for his pipe, lighting it, settling it properly in his mouth, wriggling about on the sacks, crossing his legs and spitting. Only then would he begin.

'Let it be the story of the Black Fin Water then.'

We were waiting anxiously for him to begin.

'There was once in a great city, let it be Dublin, a rich merchant and he had three sons . . .'

And so it would go on to the appointed end when the youngest and the most graceless of the three sons returned home, laden with riches. There was no morality in these stories but the absence of it was never noticed.

Once, when returning from the mill, we decided to go where an old road, now used only by carts bringing corn to the mill, twisted back to the village.

When we came in sight of the bridge over the river —
the same river that flowed so slowly and peacefully
through Paradise — we saw several of the boys from
the village school. They were standing on the
bridge, cutting rods, shouting and talking to one
another.

There was no avoiding an encounter. We could
not turn back, though if I had been alone I would
have been tempted to do so. We had been seen and
hailed with shouts of delight. We advanced slowly,
side by side, Justin bristling like a terrier dog. The
boys spread out in a line across the bridge as if to
bar the way.

When Justin came within a couple of yards of
them, he stopped. I stopped too, a foot or so behind
him. For a moment I thought there was going to
be a fight. It would not have been the first and as
yet we had never emerged the victors.

'Do you know,' said Justin sharply, 'that you are
on my grandfather's land?'

'The road's free to all,' Egan O'Doherty answered,
stepping forward. He was the undisputed leader of
the group, not because he was the tallest or strongest,
but because he was the quickest and hardiest.

'You didn't cut out those rods on the road,' Justin
went on, not budging an inch.

I looked around to see if there were any loose
stones on the roadside. To my shame be it said that
I had frequently saved myself and Justin by my
unerring aim.

Perhaps it was the knowledge that Justin was right and that they had been encroaching on our domain that caused their bellicose attitude to vanish. Egan O'Doherty smiled.

'We'll cut ye some as well.'

Justin looked past him to where one of the boys was leaning against the bridge, trimming a rod with a large jack knife.

'Would he let me use his knife?' he asked.

'Sure,' answered Egan. 'Hey, Willie! Bring over that knife and show it.'

Willie Quigley advanced, followed by the others. I stood on the outside of the circle while Justin, surrounded by the boys, felt the edge of the blade with his thumb.

'It's good enough,' he remarked, 'but mine's sharper.' And he felt in his hip pocket for his own.

'It's a girl's knife,' one of them jeered. 'No good at all.' In their envy they pressed forward to look. Justin's hand shot out to make room for himself. They retreated a step.

He pressed a knob on the side of the knife and the blade shot open. He dug it into the hazel rod which Willie held in his hand.

'See, best Sheffield steel. My grandfather bought it for me in Derry.'

They all began to speak at once. Each one wanted to handle and test the knife.

Egan O'Doherty was standing beside me on the outside of the circle. He took my hand.

'Come wi' me,' he whispered. 'I want til show ye something.'

I felt left out of all this since I had no knife to show.

'Where?' I asked.

'In under the bridge.'

I went with him. He held my arm as we slid down the bank. At the bottom he seized my ankle and placed my foot carefully on a stone. Barefoot, he stood beside me in the water, holding me perched on a stone and guiding me from one boulder to another until we reached the flat platform of rock which stretched under one side of the arch, a feat I was quite capable of performing alone and unaided. Justin was never so concerned for my safety. Beside this platform, and stretching under it, lay a deep, dark pool. I stood looking down into it, holding on to Egan's jersey. It was so dark and cold here under the bridge and my eyes were so blinded by the outer light that I could not see down into the pool.

'Has it any bottom?'

'Aye, it has, away far down. Ye could drown there.'

'Has anyone been drowned here?'

'Not that I ever heard tell on. There's a big fish down there at the bottom. He's that big.' Egan held out his arms.

'He can't be. He wouldn't fit.'

'Aye, he does. He just lies down there. Some day I'll catch him.'

'Will you? Have you ever seen him?'

41

'If ye were til lie down here and look long intil the water, ye'd see him yerself.'

'I can see nothing.' I leaned out over the edge. Egan held my right hand in his. Then suddenly he placed his left hand on the back of my neck and held me out over the water.

'Supposin' now,' he remarked quite calmly. 'Supposin' I was til push ye in.'

I felt like screaming but held back from pride.

'Ye'd be drownded, dead,' he went on.

'I wouldn't. I'd be saved.'

'There'd be none til save ye but me.' He gave me a tiny push but held on to me at the same time. I began to throw my weight back towards the wall.

'I'd be saved,' I repeated.

'Who'd save ye?' He was smiling. I was no longer afraid.

'Justin would.'

'Och, him!' The boy laughed loudly and let me go. The laugh echoed loudly under the arch. I sat down on the rock and took off my shoes and socks. I no longer believed that he would drown me. He was just showing off, but I did not trust him not to toss me into the shallow water. He hovered by my side, carrying my shoes and socks. When we got to the bank he insisted on drying my feet with his jersey and buttoning my shoes.

I found my cousin standing on the bridge with Willie's jack knife in his hand. He had exchanged it for his own.

THE years slipped into one another as a hand slips into a glove. We took no heed of their passing. Day succeeded day, each a fresh new adventure. We knew we grew bigger by our shoes and clothes but we forgot the past as quickly as we forgot our cast-off garments. Month by month, season by season, our circle of movement widened. Gradually we emerged from our narrow walled playground, and gradually we explored the narrow valley. Soon the mountains no longer closed our horizon.

One very hot day in late summer, Wattie saddled the ponies and we set off, Justin and I, on the mountain road over the shoulder of Knockdhu. It was our plan to see the sea on the other side. Justin rode Taffy, the Welsh cob, and I was mounted on Blackie, an ancient animal much more sure-footed than he appeared but of no great turn of speed. But Taffy was a lazy, over-fed beast, only too pleased to accommodate his pace to that of his elderly companion.

The stony road wound gradually higher and higher, dipping every now and then into a little valley. We passed the pleasant farm lands, the ripening fields of barley and oats, with full ears swaying and trembling gently in the light breeze, the fields of potatoes with their withering stalks. One by one we left behind us the bright, whitewashed houses, tucked comfortably under the lee of some hillock. Now and then we passed a man as he strolled along the road on his way to his fields, or a woman on her way to the village. It was the dead season between the turf digging and the harvest. The ponies when they saw a slope before them would prick up their ears and make a fine show of speed for a few minutes. But it never lasted. We ambled slowly along. Besides the road a mountain stream tumbled, its brown water leaping noisily over the stony bed. On either side the land stretched, barren moorland overgrown with heather. Here and there large granite boulders stood gleaming in the sunlight.

The sun shone down on us with blistering heat. There was no shelter in this wild land. Soon my arms in the short-sleeved sailor blouse began to burn. Justin noticed them.

'Get down, you silly ass,' he said. 'Cover your arms with mud. You'll be crying to-morrow because they hurt.'

We got down and, while I held the ponies in case they should turn round and trot home, my cousin covered my hands and arms with the gritty mud from the bank of the stream. We mounted and went on.

Farther on we came to where a bridge spanned the stream which now strayed away across the bog. Edging the ponies in to the side of the bridge wall, we leaned over the coping stones, and looked down into the deep brown pool which lay underneath. There, when our eyes became accustomed to the depth, we could see half a dozen good sized trout lying almost motionless at the bottom. We leaned over watching them in a sleepy daze. Suddenly Taffy moved on and Justin was jerked back to life.

'Look!' he cried.

I turned round and gazed ahead. Down the road a strange troop of men was coming towards us. There were some twelve of them, dressed in country-made clothes of rough home-spun flannel. They walked with a light, swinging gait and made quick unexpected gestures. Each had a red kerchief round his neck and carried an ashplant and a bundle tied up in another red handkerchief. As we came closer to this wild-looking group, so unlike the douce men of the valley, I edged Blackie in on the far side of Justin, placing my right hand on Taffy's stout flank. As we were passing them with a nod and 'Good Day', one of the men stepped up to us. His blue eyes shone in his dark face. His white teeth gleamed under his short black moustache. His hair was cut long across the forehead and cropped close over the rest of his head. He placed his hand carelessly on Taffy's bridle. My heart beat fast with fear. Were they robbers? Would they murder us? Justin sat firmly in his saddle, looking down at the smiling man. He did not smile.

' 'Tis a fine day, little gentleman,' said the man.

'Thank God,' answered Justin.

45

'Have ye travelled a long road?' asked the man again. His companions were standing idly by.

'From Glasthule.'

'Aye, a good way,' said the man, spitting on to the road. 'How many miles do ye reckon that to be?'

'A matter of six miles Irish.' My cousin jerked at Taffy's rein. But the man had a firm grip on the bridle.

'Steady, young fella. Ye've no call til be afeared.'

'I'm not,' answered my cousin in a low even voice.

'I'll take my oath ye're not.' The man wagged his head gravely. 'What call would ye have til be afeared riding the roads, you and yer lovely sister.'

'She is my cousin.' Justin never moved in the saddle nor raised his eyes from the man.

'Is she now?' He shifted his gaze from my cousin to me. 'What do they call ye, lass?'

'Anne-Louise,' I answered, nervously.

'A fine name, a noble name! Are ye strangers to these parts?'

'We live with our grandfather. His name is Thorauld.'

'So ye're Mr. Thorauld's grandchilder. A fine man, yer granddad, a fine gentleman.'

'And who might you be?' asked Justin.

'Just poor harvesters, we come from beyond, from the townland of Glenbawn. We're on our way to Scotland, looking for work.'

'Scotland! That's a long way off. How are you going to get there?'

'We'll walk as far as Derry and there we'll get the Glesga boat. After that we're in God's hands.'

'What's Scotland like?' asked Justin, curious because on clear days we could see Scotland lying far out on the north-east horizon.

'A cold black country,' said the man, shaking his head sadly. 'A country where the birds have forgotten til sing and the neighbour doesn't stand at his door til welcome ye in. Anyways that's how it was where I worked.'

'Why do you go then?'

The man looked round him at the wild barren hills. He threw out his arm with a broad sweep, embracing the whole wide horizon.

'There's little can grow here. And it has pleased the Almighty til give us mouths. Isn't it a queer thing when ye come til think of it? Everything that God gives us seems til have two uses. We sing, we talk, we laugh wi' our mouths, but we must needs eat wi' them too. And our hands that love til touch the smooth neck of a horse, our hands must needs handle a spade or delve in the clabber, or maybe be cut til pieces by the sheet in a storm.' He held out his hands. The palms were seared with scars which ran across them like burns.

'Why do they not speak to us?' asked Justin, nodding towards the other men.

They were seated now by the roadside, talking together in low voices. One of them had lit a clay pipe and was passing it round. Another had broken off a piece of oatcake he carried in his bundle and was chewing it.

'They feel strange, and forbye they have little English. I've been in Scotland before. But will ye not stop a while and eat wi' us?'

Justin shook his head.

'We're riding on over Knockdhu and want to be home before nightfall.'

The man raised his face to the sky.

'Ye'd best be going home now, for a storm's comin'.'

Justin laughed: 'On a day like this?'

'Aye,' the man waved his hand. 'If ye knew the signs of the sky as I do, ye'd turn yer horses' heads and make for home. I've seen the heaviest clouds gather in a clear sky and I've seen waves like mountains rise up on a sea as flat as the palm of yer hand.'

'I think we'll go on,' answered Justin, who was difficult to turn from his set path. 'It doesn't matter much anyway. We're used to weather.' He gave Taffy's rein a tug. The man released the bridle and lifting his arm, cried out:

'Fortune attend ye. May the road lie smooth before ye.'

The others called after us. My cousin answered them in the small Gaelic he had picked up. Over our shoulders we watched them rise, first one, then two or three, then all of them and go down the hill. As they went one of them began to sing a melancholy song. They disappeared in a hollow of the road.

On and on we went. At last we arrived at the head of the pass. We looked back and saw the land stretched out below us like a patchwork quilt, the brown moors, the coloured fields of the low-lying farms, the shining water of the bay winding out to sea and far away the great black bens. Beyond the bay lay the ridge of hills which led to Fanad. Out to sea, on the distant horizon, the smoke of a passing steamer drifted.

Justin sniffed the air and looked toward the south-west.

'See, the man was right. The storm's coming.'

'Shall we turn back?'

Justin shook his head.

'We'll get wet anyway, I doubt. I know there's no house nearer than MacNeil's on this side. Maybe we might find one on the far side.'

I shook my head but followed him. The road lay downhill now. The ponies, as if they could smell the coming storm, set off at a jog trot, Taffy pulling hard on his rein. We rode on for a couple of miles without speaking. The clouds were gathering round the sun and over the whole country a darkness fell. The wind began to creep up, first softly, then with a boisterous harshness. The first peal of thunder began to rumble through the mountains.

There was no stream here. The road, like a causeway, lay some twelve feet above the surrounding bog, a dark treacherous bog, full of cut banks and deep holes. It was the last place where one could expect to find a human habitation.

Suddenly the road twisted round a spur of the mountain. Far away, folded between hills, lay the eastern sea, the Sea of Moyle, like a sheet of steel, and in the far distance a faint blue line, already obscured by the clouds, the coast of Scotland. This was what we had come to see but we did not tarry to look at it. The first drops of rain were already beating on our backs and the heavy roll of thunder broke sharp and crackling above us. The ponies shied at the lightning. We looked right and left. Then we saw, behind a rise, the blue smoke of a chimney. Justin was for turning the ponies straight across the bog towards it.

It was now my turn to be obstinate. I was always afraid of the bogs.

'No, Justin, no!' I urged. 'It's dangerous. We don't know the ground. We might get into a bog-hole. Best go round by the road. There'll be a lane somewhere.'

Impatiently Justin jerked Taffy's head and we jogged along down the rainswept road. About a quarter of a mile farther along we came to the lane. It was nothing more than a rough track, a stone path across the boggy land. Beaten sore by the rain, which was now mixed with hail, we urged on the ponies and after a little twisting and turning we came in sight of the house.

It was a low, whitewashed, three-roomed cottage with a thatched roof, scratched by the hens. Tufts of grass grew at the chimney corners and the roughly cobbled yard was covered with mud. The midden lay just in front of the door. Near it were a few poor fields of potatoes and barley.

We were greeted by the barking of dogs, lean, high-backed greyhounds; they snapped and snarled at our heels, causing Taffy to rear. Even Blackie, who as a rule paid no attention to dogs, began to turn round in circles. An old woman, in a red petticoat with a white mutch on her head and a shawl hastily thrown round her shoulders, rushed out of the door and waved her apron at them, calling them by name. They slunk back into the house. The old woman came close up to us, peering closely into our faces.

'Come along in, childer,' she cried in a high piercing voice. 'Come in out of the rain.'

We tied the ponies to a post, unsaddled them as quickly as possible and staggered under the weight of the saddles into the house. The old woman waited for us in the doorway and pushed us into the kitchen in front of her, fussing all the time.

'You're drownded, my lambs, drownded. Sit close up til the fire there and dry yerselves. I'll get ye a drink of milk.'

The door closed against the summer storm, the kitchen was dark. What little daylight there was came through a small four-paned window, and most of this was taken up by a geranium in a pot. Beneath the window stood a table and beside the table, in the dark, sat an old man who slowly became visible to our eyes, unaccustomed to the dimness of the room. He sat in a high wooden chair, his head erect, his feet resting on a footstool. His thick white hair hung across his forehead, meeting his heavy white brows. His forked beard fell white as snow over his broad chest. He was dressed in the saffron kilt one saw so seldom now and by his chair rested his pipes. We knew now where we were. This was the house of O'Cahan, the piper. His name was known far and near, and though nowadays he seldom stirred abroad, we often heard of him. Scholars and musicians came to visit him. But in spite of all they would say he refused to leave his mountainy home where his ancestors had been driven by the planters. Like so many they had refused to become peasants. They earned their bread as horse-dealers, dog-breeders, tinkers, anything rather than plough the land they had once owned for the profit of another.

The old man leaned forward in his chair, his gnarled hands grasping the wooden arms, his gleaming eyes fixed on our faces. Then he shouted something in Gaelic to the old woman who had gone down into the 'room' to fetch us some food. She bustled back. Justin had risen to his feet and was looking at old O'Cahan, a puzzled frown on his brow. Our knowledge of Gaelic was confined to a few phrases. The old woman turned to Justin apologetically and said in a low voice:

'Don't pay any heed to him, my dear. He's old now and strange in his ways. He's asking who ye might be.'

Justin looked steadily at old O'Cahan and replied:

'I am Justin Thorauld and this is my cousin Anne-Louise Delahaie. We are grandchildren of Mr. Thorauld of Glasthule.'

The old man nodded solemnly.

'You are welcome.'

That much at least we understood and replied:

'A thousand thanks.'

'He's very old now,' the woman went on. 'He was a great man in his day, tall and soople as a poplar tree. But he's failing badly now. He now talks only Irish.'

'How old is he?' asked Justin.

'No one rightly knows, but he minds the bad times. He was a young man then.'

'Our grandfather was a little boy then. But he'll never talk about them.'

The old woman shook her head:

'And small wonder. Few will. Death itself stalked the land. In the whole valley no smoke rose.'

The storm was passing over. A beam of sunlight struck through the window, lighting up the pale leaves of the geranium. We were too well versed in the good manners of the countryside to rise up and go, now that we had accepted hospitality. Justin, however, made the usual polite remark.

'We'd best be getting along now.'

'No, no, my lambs, no. Take yer ease. Soon Jamie will be home and he'll show ye a short cut over the bog. Wait a wee while, ye must be weary.'

We waited, saying nothing, gazing around us at the kitchen, furnished barely with table and stools, at the great bed in the corner with its red curtains, at the old man seated in the chair. He sat there so quiet and still that he seemed asleep. Only his dark eyes, as bright as those of a bird, watched us with a dark unwinking stare.

I remembered my manners:

'How many children have you?' I asked.

'I had five, five brave sons, tall and strong.' The old woman began to sway backwards and forwards. 'But they're all gone now, God rest their souls. Two of the fever, one at sea and two in the bloody wars. There's none left now but my two grandsons. They should be back now. They've taken shelter, likely, from the storm.'

Lest she should begin, as old people have a way of doing, to describe the end of each son, Justin hastened to ask:

'From where do you come yourself and who are your people?'

'I come from the nine glens. But that was a long while past. Since that day I've had no people but him.'

A shadow passed the window and we could hear steps on the cobbled yard. The door opened and two young men came in. They stooped as they passed over the threshold. The taller of them was carrying a heavy stone jar. Tall, lean and agile, with thick black curly hair, the freckles stood out on his pale skin like rain-drops on the window-pane. His brother was shorter, more thick-set and strongly built. The old woman looked up and rattled out a stream of words quite incomprehensible to us. The young man stood looking at us and then slipped away down into the room.

'They've been down the road to MacGonigle's shop to get me some oil. They're good boys and kind to the old people.'

There was no lamp in the room.

When Jamie came back he and his brother lifted the great pot of potatoes which hung over the fire and brought it out to the yard. They came back with the potatoes steaming in a basket which they placed on the hearth. The old woman put the best of them on a wooden platter in the centre of the table. Then she placed knives and forks and plates with a bowl of buttermilk for each. There was no going away now. We would have to stay and eat.

'Now, my lambs,' she said. 'Draw over to the table. It's poor but wholesome and will help ye on yer road back home.'

It would have been impolite to refuse. Also we were hungry. But before we ate the two young men took, one a plate of potatoes and salt, the other a bowl of what smelled to our practised noses suspiciously like whisky. They approached the old man and kneeling down on one knee each in turn said:

'Eat, O'Cahan!'

'Drink, O'Cahan!'

The old man took the food and drink silently from his grandsons and set it on the table beside him. We all ate, dipping our potatoes in the salt and washing them down with sour buttermilk. When the meal was over we made ready to depart. As we said good-bye, old O'Cahan took Justin's hand and passing his other over my head, said in English:

'You are welcome to my house. Come again.'

Jamie saddled the ponies and we set out across the bog. The old woman stood at the door, waving her apron in farewell. Jamie walked beside Blackie, holding the bridle lest the old pony should stumble. Justin followed. The air was cool and fresh after the storm, the sunlight glittered on the bog-pools and the smell of the boggy earth rose around us. Jamie started to whistle and then sing a song.

'What tune is that?' asked Justin.

'It's a tune my grandad had when he was a young man from a dark poet that walked the roads of Galway. It's called Ballylea.'

'Will you be a poet and a piper too?'

Jamie threw back his head and laughed:

'Indeed no, there's nothing to be gained by piping old tunes til them as won't hear. When next spring comes, I'll be getting along out of here. The old man won't likely over the winter. Then my brother is gettin' married and there'll be no room for me.'

'Where will you go, to Scotland?'

'Not Scotland. It's colder there than here. I want to go where there's sun and life. Once when I was in Derry selling a couple of dogs, I fell in wi' a sailor man. He stood wi' his back to a wall, shiverin' in the rain, and he told me stories of where he came from, down below in South America. The sun always shines there and the rivers are so broad, ye can't see the other side, and the trees are so tall ye can't see the top branches, and there is food there for everyone. There are cities there, the like ye wouldn't find the whole world over. Since that day there's been a great longing on me to go there.'

'We'll go there too. Maybe some day we'll meet. But don't you want to come back? I do.'

Jamie looked over his shoulder at my cousin.

'What would there be til come back for? Hunger and darkness. There isn't here what would keep a crow alive. I can't see myself sitting waiting for death like the old man.'

'I shall come back,' said Justin.

We reached the point where the path joined the road. Jamie stood in the gap looking after us as we rode off. When we came to the turn of the road he lifted his arm and shouted after us. Justin leaned back and shouted in reply.

As we jogged along I said:

'That couldn't have been oil in that jar. They didn't have any lamp in the house.'

'It wasn't oil.'

'What do you think it was?'

'Poteen.'

'Why do you think they wouldn't tell us the truth?'

'They were afraid we might say something to grandfather.'

'Shall we?'

'No,' shouted my cousin.

All that summer and autumn we wandered far afield, often not returning before nightfall. Aunt Molly never worried. She knew some kindly farmer's wife would feed us. What friends we made lived far from the village. A wandering herd, a travelling man on his rounds with his pack full of needles and thread, a lazy farm-boy watching the cows at pasture and making a basket of osiers, these were our friends and companions.

Our favourite hunting ground was the great black cliffs which lay beyond the bar at the entrance to the little bay. Here when the tide was out, the rock pools would be full of all sorts of small animals, scurrying hither and thither in fright when we cast our shadow over the water. We liked to lie on the brink and drop grains of sand into the sea-anemones to watch them gather their delicate tendrils together in hope of a meal. We would lift rocks to see the crabs sidle forth, rattling over the stones and coarse gravel in their effort to find a new hiding-place. We used to climb up the cliffs and lean over to watch the seagulls in their nests. Over our heads the parent birds would wheel, shrieking angrily, coming nearer and nearer until they almost flew into our faces and we could look into their cruel yellow eyes, hungry unwinking eyes, and at last drive us away.

It was after a storm that the cliffs were at their best. During a storm it was impossible to go there, but when the wind dropped the sea would rise as if released from the binding anger of the tempest and would lash itself against the cliffs, sending the spray far inland. One could see it lie in flecks of foam on the ploughed land, in the furrows of which the sea-gulls would cower, looking for food which the sea denied. Then when the sea too had gone down, except for a low growling, we would clamber down the clefts which seamed the cliffs and walk along the tide line. All sorts of strange fish would lie dead on the edge of the water. We turned them over with curiosity and buried them in the rough gravel or sand which lay between the boulders. To jelly-fish we paid little attention. Even when alive, and the sea was often full of them, we did not really regard them as creatures, because of their immobility. Starfish lay glistening in the sunlight and sea-urchins in their delicate spiky shells. Often a dead bird, its wings outstretched, its neck and legs stark, would call forth cries of pity. And over all the black shags and the ravenous seagulls would wheel and dive, looking for the fish which had been scared into the depths of the sea and had not yet dared to rise to the surface.

One day after such a storm Justin and I wandered forth, crossed the sandhills and came to the bens. It was the time of the Easter holidays and we were not alone out here. Some of the village boys had come down before us to hunt for crabs for their supper. We came to where the path wound down the great cleft in the rock and there below us we saw them, gathered together in a noisy group. They had a long line and at the end of the line there was a seagull on a hook. They had caught it by throwing a bait out into the water and were playing it like a trout. Back and forward the bird darted, sometimes let fly a bit and then dragged back. The boys screamed with delight and the seagull screamed with rage and alarm.

Justin's face went very white. He clenched his fists and made towards the path. I caught hold of his coat and held him.

'What are you going to do?' I cried.

'Kill them,' he answered.

'They'll kill *you*,' I cried. 'Look, there are a dozen of them down there. They'll hammer you to death.'

I held on to the coat. Justin sat down full of fury. He looked down at the boys who now had the sea-gull in their hands. They went down to the water's edge. The tide was out. They tethered the bird there and left it. They came back towards the cliff face, presumably to watch the dying struggles of the bird as the water rose higher round it.

'Let me go!' shouted my cousin.

'Come away,' I cried, almost in tears and lying on the edge of the coat to give myself better leverage.

'Let me go!' he repeated, undoing the buttons of the coat and slipping out of it.

He did not go down the cliff. He stood there at the top of the path, watching the boys. They began to climb the path, slowly for it was steep and dangerous. Then I saw what Justin intended to do. He was standing beside a large boulder, balanced at the edge of the cleft. He began to push. I rushed at him again. I tore at his collar but he merely kicked me off. Then I ran to the edge and began to shout and wave to the boys below. They could not hear my words and waved back. My legs lost their strength, I could not move a step. I could only wave my arms and go on screaming. Justin's face was no longer pale. It was red with exertion and his eyes bloodshot and furious. The rock swayed, tottered and finally fell over. It bounded forward with a horrible noise bringing other stones and rocks with it. The boys saw it coming. Those at the bottom of the cliff jumped back. One or two who were already on the path flattened themselves against the side of the cliff and escaped. But one boy who had advanced too far to go back or take shelter was caught. It was Egan O'Doherty. The rocks hit him and passed on. He rolled to the bottom and lay there, white and still.

Still I could not move. I was certain that the boy was dead, that Justin had killed him. I stood watching my cousin and trembled all over as if I were in a fever. Slowly he took up his jacket and put it on. Then he went down the cliff, slowly and carefully, down into the middle of those boys, now clustered round their comrade. He passed them. They made no attempt to touch him, though they shouted at him and shook their fists. He went on, down to the tide's edge where he untied the seagull, which clawed and tore at him with its beak and claws, and set it free. For a moment it lay there, opening and shutting its beak, flapping round with its wings, then suddenly it rose and sailed away towards the farther cliffs.

While I was watching him, a boy called John Elkin passed me. He was going for help. As he ran past he stopped and looked at me. His dark face was savage with fear and rage.

'He'll hang,' he shouted at me triumphantly. 'And you'll hang wi' him.'

These words seemed to bring me to my senses. The trembling stopped and I began to think what we should do. Justin had turned round and was coming back. I armed myself with some stones to protect him if necessary. But no defence was needed. The boys let him pass. Something of another world had already attached itself to him in their eyes. They could see the hangman's rope round his neck. He climbed up the path and came to where I was standing.

'We'd better go home and tell grandfather,' I said. 'Perhaps he can save you.'

'I hope he's dead,' answered my cousin.

Just then John Elkin came back, accompanied by a shepherd. The man knew us well, though we did not know his name. He went down and fetched up the boy. It was a hard job even for a man accustomed to heavy work, but I suppose he had frequently had to carry a sheep up this path. He dropped Egan from his shoulders at the top of the cliff and said to us:

'He's not dead. You'd better get home before worse happens and ask someone to go for the doctor.'

We set off, the boys following slowly. Justin would not be hurried. I wanted to run all the way but he refused to hasten his step. He walked along, very pale and grim, not speaking. I kept saying:

'Come on, Justin. Hurry. Let's get home quickly.'

I felt that the only person who could save us from a lifetime spent behind prison walls or a ghastly, shameful death, was grandfather. Justin was deaf to my urgings.

When I saw the grey walls of grandfather's house I left him and ran towards it. Still he did not hasten. I rushed round through the yard, in through the kitchen, past Bella who was standing with the

63

gridiron in her hand. Along the passage, without waiting to take off my shoes and coat, and into the small sitting-room. There on one side of the fire sat grandfather smoking his pipe and reading. On the other sat Aunt Molly, sewing. I flung myself on grandfather's knees, crying:

'Justin, Grandfather, save him.'

Aunt Molly threw down her sewing, came forward and tried to lift me up. But I clung all the tighter to my grandfather.

'What is the matter, dear?' she asked. 'What has happened to Justin?'

'He'll be put in prison, he'll be hanged,' I sobbed.

Grandfather put his pipe in the rack and took me on his knees. I was a big girl now and didn't fit there any longer. I sobbed against his shoulder.

'He's nearly killed Egan O'Doherty. He's nearly killed him.'

'Hush, dear,' said Aunt Molly. 'Tell us quietly. Things can't be so bad. Don't be so upset.'

'He pushed a rock down on Egan O'Doherty. He lay there. He looked dead,' I shouted, hardly aware that I was shouting.

'Where is Justin now?' grandfather asked quietly.

'Coming,' I gasped through my sobs.

Just then Justin's step could be heard in the back hall. He was taking off his coat and shoes before coming in. I listened, trembling. How could he be so cool? The door opened and he came in. He walked straight up to grandfather and said:

'I'm afraid I have hurt Egan O'Doherty rather badly, sir.'

His voice sounded shrill. He kept his hands in his pockets.

Grandfather looked at him quietly without getting up. Then leaning forward he grasped him by the shoulder and said:

'You had better stay here while I go and see what has to be done and find the doctor. He is probably only slightly hurt. We must look after him. You had better have something to eat.'

He went out.

Justin sat down, white and silent. I went on sobbing against Aunt Molly. Justin looked at me, fury in his eyes.

'He deserved it,' he muttered furiously. 'He deserved it, the cruel beast.'

The door opened and Bella came in to find out what was the matter, carrying a basket of turf we did not need.

'Bella,' said Aunt Molly, 'bring the children in some hot soup and bread.'

The food came in on a tray. I choked as I tried to eat my soup and to my amazement Justin ate his greedily as if nothing had happened. Suddenly I became a little afraid of my cousin.

Grandfather brought home better news. Egan was suffering from slight concussion. His head had been badly cut but it was not dangerous. The doctor was with him and said that no bones had been broken. 'So far so good,' grandfather remarked. But then, as the boy was reported out of danger, resentment began to run high in the village. The respect in which my grandfather was held prevented any strong expression of feeling, but everyone was saying that Justin would have to be punished. No one wanted an open scandal, but everyone wanted the assurance that grandfather had dealt with the matter in a firm manner. It was well known that grandfather objected to corporal punishment and it was this leniency which was blamed for the incident.

Grandfather said nothing at the time beyond reassuring us and quieting my fright. But he talked the matter over with Aunt Molly. We knew from the fact that Aunt Molly's eyes were very red and the general air of strain that there was something in the wind. Justin went about with a grim look on his face. He wandered about the fields and gardens, doing nothing, because grandfather had forbidden us the village and the shore. We began to feel outcasts from our fellow-men. They were the dreariest days I ever remember. Aunt Molly tried to invent tasks for us, but there was so little to do at this time of the year, no weeding, no fruit-picking, that most of the time we were idle. We were too upset to read.

Then grandfather called us into his sitting-room. He sat there smiling, his pipe in his mouth.

'I am sorry,' he said, 'that you have been having

a bad time, but I could not let you know what was going to happen until I had heard from Justin's father. You see, Justin, no one can take the law into his own hands without suffering for it. I know that what you did was done in a spirit of indignation against cruelty, but it is more important to realize that poverty is the cause of cruelty than to punish it. The one immediate result of this act of yours is that the people of the village have become afraid of you and consequently they feel angry with you. You have to go away. As it happens you were to have gone to school in the autumn. This only hastens our parting a little. I have a letter from your father. You will be leaving for England next week. That's all now, except, of course, to say that I hope you will come back to see me from time to time and always let me know what you are doing. I shall always be interested. You are not only my grandson, you are also my pupil.'

The days preceding Justin's departure were days of misery. Deep gloom settled on the old house. It could be felt even in the kitchen. Bella's sprightly sallies almost ceased. Theresa, overcome by one of her mad fits, ran home. Aunt Molly wept openly. Every now and then she broke down and cried:

'This is the worst of bringing up other people's children. You love them as if they were your own and then they are taken from you.'

Justin and I felt acutely miserable. There was nothing we could do to soothe her grief. Listlessly

67

we pottered in and out of the house, sighing with boredom.

Even grandfather was not himself. His manner became curt and every day we feared to find his study door locked. He sat by the fireside smoking or playing the flute or reading the well-thumbed volumes of Pascal and Lucretius which always lay to hand.

At night Justin and I no longer made plans for the conquest of the world. I listened carefully while he gave me instructions with regard to his animals and property. His books were going with him, all but the few he no longer wanted. These he had generously given to me, tearing out his own name and writing mine.

'Listen, Loulie,' he'd say. 'You must remember to feed the cat. Bella will forget. And stop her from throwing the potstick at him when she's annoyed. Be sure you clean out the rabbit hutches every morning and give the rabbits green leaves. Put a saucer of milk in the garden for the hedgehogs and change the water in the bird bath. When the blackbird's wing is better, let him fly away.'

These instructions he repeated every night as if he were afraid I might forget. On the last night he added:

'And when you are taken away, be sure to get Manus to look after the animals that might still be here. Bring them over to the mill.'

'But I'm not going away.'

'Of course you will,' he said sharply. 'They'll send you to school too. Girls' schools are even worse than boys'. Won't I be sorry for you. You can't stay here all your life.'

Then as if to lighten my grief at this evil prospect, he added:

'I'll come for you later on and we'll go off together. When we're old like grandfather and Aunt Molly, we'll come back here to live.'

Next morning grandfather called Justin into his study and gave him as a parting gift a new volume of Pascal's *Pensées* and an old French Bible. He kissed him on both cheeks and shook hands. Then grandfather and I stood in front of the house and waved good-bye as Aunt Molly and Justin drove off.

Wattie flicked the whip over Dick's head and called over his shoulders:

'Have ye a hould, Miss Molly?'

Dick pranced restively and then bolted off down the village street. Justin leaned back, waving his handkerchief until the old phaeton wheeled past the forge, across the bridge and disappeared in a cloud of dust.

Grandfather and I turned back into the house, each silent and alone. The house seemed like a church after service, quiet and filled with ghostly beings.

My cousin Justin had gone out into the world.

PART II

DOWN IN THE LAGAN

THE Lagan is a rich country, a land of broad valleys and small wooded hills, of heavy soil and wide, slow-moving rivers. The broad acres of the fields yield full crops. You do not see here the sparse barley corner nor the stone-wall enclosure of potatoes. There are no fierce winds to lay low the corn, no heavy rains to beat down the flax-pods, no storms to tear up the apple-trees in the orchards. The farmers hereabouts are strong, full-bellied men, gloomy and taciturn, as befits their prosperity. No room in their bellies for wind, they say. Their pride is all in their wide acres, their lush grasslands and their flax. Only rich land can bear flax.

In summer when the smell of the retting flax lies heavy over the land, you can see them, standing in groups of two or three, scarce passing a word between them, looking now at the sky, now around them at their fields, weighing, measuring and considering. They open their nostrils wide and draw deep into their lungs the pungent, sickly-sweet odour. It smells sweeter to them than all the perfumes of Araby. There is no land which can grow such flax as theirs, nowhere else can such linen be woven, linen thread as fine as silk and as strong as a steel cable.

Yet they are uneasy men, at times frightened men. Generation after generation they have been reminded unpleasantly that they are planters, have no rightful claim. When they raise their eyes to the distant mountains, they remember the lean men who have been dispossessed, hungry men with long memories. They see them at the hiring fairs, they see them at work in their fields and each says to himself: 'I wonder when this fellow will come along with a pike or a gun.' They hear their hired men and girls talk in a language they do not understand, and from lack of understanding, hate. They hear them sing songs of victory and defeat, of death and glory. They remember the stories of Phelim Roe and Count O'Hanlon, of Moonlighters and the Break o' Day Boys. They are ever on the watch. They know in their bones that some day these hungry hands will seize their lands, their flax-pits, their scutching mills and weaving-mills. If not to-day, then to-morrow.

WHEN my father gave up coffee planting in Java and returned home, on the death of my mother's cousin, he took over the family linen mills. Shortly afterwards I left my grandfather's house and went to live with my parents. My mother was greatly shocked at my wild appearance, rough manners and country accent. She was a tall, boney woman, with beautiful dark red hair and the red-brown eyes that go with it. She looked at me as if I were a changeling and suddenly all the romantic love I had stored up for her withered away. I clung to Aunt Molly who did not want to lose me. Aunt Molly urged another year or two of open-air life before I began school, but my mother was firm. I must be properly educated, taught to be a lady and my accent corrected. Aunt Molly resented these remarks deeply and retorted with a sharpness of which I did not think her capable, that ladies were born and not made and she saw nothing wrong with me. Her own accent was not above reproach.

My mother raised her thin eyebrows.

'She is a little savage, Molly, and she talks like a peasant. She ought to be sent to school in England if she is ever to speak decently.'

'She's a nice child and, thank God, a healthy child, and you should be thankful. What harm is it that she has an Irish accent? It's better than mincing her words anyway.'

The smirk that so disfigured my mother's handsome face and which I came to loathe, now passed across her features.

'I know you've been very good to her, Molly, and taken good care of her. But after all she's my child and I know what is best for her. You should have married and had children of your own.'

Aunt Molly flushed to the roots of her hair with anger. Then there broke out between the two women the most horrible row I had ever heard. Up to now I had been surrounded with love and sympathy and I could not understand why two human beings should deliberately rage at one another, but young as I was, I felt the insult that had been thrown at Aunt Molly. I fled to the kitchen and in spite of Bella's comforting I cried as if my heart were broken. I wept intermittently until we left the next day. Grandfather mysteriously absented himself from the sisterly altercation.

My mother packed my clothes with disgust, saying every now and then:

'Your aunt has strange ideas of what is becoming in a lady,' and:

'Your aunt should know better than to let you wear shoes like that. You'll grow up with thick ankles.'

I felt myself included in the condemnation of Aunt Molly and I was given to feel, too, that I was a great clumsy ugly girl. It was years before I realized that I was really rather small and delicately built.

I was terribly lonely in my new home. My mother and father were strangers to me and I thoroughly disliked my two sisters. They formed an alliance against me, keeping me out of their games and falling silent if I joined them. Soon I left them alone. I was older and their childish prattle rather bored me, so I did not keep up the effort to make friends with them. When I once complained to my mother of my loneliness, she replied coldly:

'You have your sisters to play with.'

My mother did not get her way, however, about my education. My father saw no sense in sending me away to school just yet. There was a good school in the town and he never liked spending money except for his own comfort or greater glory. My mother could correct my accent herself. This she did continuously, but though she succeeded in eliminating certain words and phrases from my speech she never managed to change my accent. She mocked at me, imitated me, scolded me, but she only roused a fierce obstinacy which remains with me to this day.

In the autumn I was sent to school. I was delighted to go, to meet other girls of my own age and perhaps make friends. I was anxious to learn. I had the idea that other girls of my age knew a great deal more than I did. But I was disappointed. I made no friends. The girls of my own social class were sent to boarding schools or had governesses and here I met the daughters of rich farmers and the better-off tradesmen. I did not walk to school or cycle, I was driven there in the trap and was called for again in the afternoon. My mother insisted on this. At the same time I was one of the worst dressed children in the school. At grandfather's it had not mattered what I wore. Although my mother criticized my aunt's taste, she had none herself and I always looked shabby. The other girls took care to point this out. It was impossible to make friends with them. I was shy of them and they distrusted me. So more and more I was driven back on myself and back on my books.

Occasionally I got a letter from Justin but for some reason my mother disliked our corresponding. Now I know that she was angry that she had no son and did not wish me to have a brother of whom she was not the mother. At any rate we were both at an age when writing letters is a difficult business, so except at Christmas and on birthdays we rarely heard from one another.

It was while I was at school that the Ulster Volunteer Movement began, a movement which sprang out of double fear, fear of the native Catholic Irish, oppressed for centuries and now since the days of Parnell asserting themselves more and more, and the more tangible fear of the workers. As usual it was the less real fear that was emphasized. The factory owners, the ship-builders, the newspapers and the bourgeoisie declared with every breath they took that Home Rule was Rome Rule, and the worker was for the hundredth time deceived. The terror spread from the bourgeoisie to the farmer, always in fear of losing his land. The humour of the country changed. The Catholics went in fear and the Protestants, belligerent and boastful, shouted their defiance against Rome, Ireland and the Crown. In the mills the Catholic worker and the Protestant worker looked at each other with mistrust and hatred.

In the evening one would meet groups of men and boys, marching along the road, playing soldiers, or factory girls sauntering home from the mill, the tow still in their hair, singing old party songs according to their persuasion. If trouble broke out in a factory, the owner had only to dismiss a few Catholic work-men for the old feud to break out and feeling be turned from himself. Hatred lay heavy on the land like the reek of flax in July.

My father was a Liberal and disliked the whole business. My mother, on the contrary, sympathized. She enjoyed attending committee meetings and gatherings where the women of her class received instruction in first aid and made bandages. It may have been partly owing to her influence that my father grudgingly subscribed to the funds of the movement, but I think it is more likely that it was because he began to receive letters threatening to burn down his mill. He was forced to temporize with the powers of darkness and this made him all the more violent against them in private.

One evening a neighbouring mill-owner dropped

79

in and stayed to dinner. My father was in one of his worst moods. That day a Protestant foreman had struck a Catholic worker and it looked as if trouble might break out in the mill. He grumbled loudly.

'Look here, Edgington, you're one of the men most responsible in this district for all this trouble,' he said. 'You've let the devil himself loose. Where's it all going to end? Civil War?'

'No, Delahaie, it will never come to that. We'll force Asquith to shelve the Home Rule Bill.'

'And if the others kick?'

'They won't kick against the might of the British Empire.'

'Haven't you thought that the British Army might be turned against you?'

'We've seen to that,' Mr. Edgington replied with a grin.

My father let that pass. It was only too well known that a certain class supported the Ulster Movement in England.

'But what good will it do us if the Bill is shelved?'

'If we have Home Rule, Delahaie, we are ruined.'

'That's rot. You don't believe any more than I do in this cry of Home Rule. You know our trade — the linen trade — doesn't lie with England. We sell in the States.'

'Look at it like this. If Home Rule comes, the ship-building goes, and if ship-building goes, linen goes. It's a subsidiary industry.'

'The ship-building won't go.'

'It will. It will go to the Clyde. It may be just a matter of opinion, but I am sure that if Ireland is separated from England, the English will build their boats on the Tyne and on the Clyde. But we won't argue the point. There's another aspect of the case, one you have obviously not carefully considered. You know as well as I do that linen won't pay if we have to pay the same wages to our workers as, say, the Lancashire mill-owners pay theirs. If the unions get strong in Ulster, we might as well close shop. Cotton will drive us off the market. There must be no solidarity between the Catholic and the Protestant worker. The prosperity of Ulster depends on that.'

'You mean our prosperity.'

'Aren't we Ulster?'

'Neither Ulster nor Ireland,' said my father.

My mother thought it wise to change the subject.

My father was determined that I should be neither coaxed nor coerced into taking part in the movement. When my mother suggested that I should accompany her to her first aid classes, he shouted with rage, and banged his fist on the table. He could not, he declared, prevent my mother from making a fool of herself, but she was not going to make one of his daughter. I was grateful to him. Brought up as I had been in a Catholic village, this religious bigotry horrified me.

School was but a reflection of what was going on in the outside world. At first I was regarded as a brand to be snatched from the burning, then abandoned as a renegade. I am afraid that I said many things which would have counted against my father if the Great War had not broken out.

It fell on us out of a clear summer sky. Before we realized what had happened, the boys who had played at being soldiers were soldiers in earnest. From the plough, the mills, the shipyards, from the four provinces of Ireland they went. How many returned?

Aunt Molly wrote to tell me that Justin had joined the army. At first I could not believe it. It was difficult to think of Justin as grown up. But of course he was two years older than I was, just nineteen. I wrote to him. He replied; one of those brief epistles I received from time to time.

'Dear Loulie,

'Here I am in this goddamned camp learning to hunt the Hun. The life's rough but pleasant enough and I am near enough London to get up sometimes. Could you come over? We could have a good time together for a few days. I'd like to see you again. Aunt Molly tells me you are a bit of a brain and that you are planning to go to Trinity College, Dublin, in the autumn. I hope you like it better than I did Oxford. Good luck and all the best.

'Your loving cousin,
Justin.'

One morning that autumn I came down to breakfast and found my mother crying and reading a letter. I glanced quickly at the envelope lying on her plate and my heart stopped beating for a moment. The letter was from Aunt Molly. What could have happened? I sat down without asking. There was nothing to be gained by saying anything to my mother. If it pleased her to do so, she would keep the information from me all day. She folded the letter, sighed, put it back into the envelope and began to pour out the tea. My father came in, sat down at the foot of the table and opened the morning paper.

'Redmond was speaking in Dublin yesterday,' he remarked.

'Why doesn't he send all those fellows down there to the Front?' my mother replied with an audible sniff.

My father looked up.

'What's the matter?' he asked.

'It's horrible,' my mother answered tearfully and indignantly. 'It's really horrible. My own sister and she behaves like this.'

'What the hell's the matter?' shouted my father, his temper rising. He could never be patient with my mother's procrastinations. As usual she was quite unmoved. She never paid any attention to my father's temper until it broke forth in all its force. Then she retired to her room and wept.

'I've no idea why she should treat me like this. I have always been so thoughtful. It really grieves me to find my own sister so inconsiderate of my feelings. Anyone would think he was not my father.'

My father's fist came down full force on the table. My two sisters looked pale and frightened.

'She has sent for Loulie,' my mother explained with dignity. 'I think that it was her duty to send for me. She seems to think I have no natural feelings. Loulie can't go, she has her work to do.'

'In the name of God, woman,' roared my father, 'what is the matter? Why has Loulie been sent for?'

'Martin,' said my mother. 'The servants will hear you.'

'Will you tell me what has happened? Give me that letter!'

'Father is dying,' my mother answered through her tears.

'Well, in that case, Loulie has got to go. He has probably sent for her. She can take her books with her.'

'Why should he want to see his granddaughter and not his daughter? I'm sure Molly has been making mischief again. She wants to have everything for herself.'

'I don't care,' shouted my father over the top of his newspaper. 'Keep your quarrels with your sister to yourself. Loulie can go.'

When I arrived at the small wayside station, there was a bitterly cold wind blowing, and cold drops of rain, mixed with sleet, struck my face. I looked around, but there was no sign of Aunt Molly. But standing forlorn and sad beside the ticket office I saw Wattie. He had not felt sure of being able to

84

recognize me and was waiting for me to come to him. He looked aged and shrivelled under his coat.

'Don't you know me, Wattie?' I asked, seizing his arm.

He shook my hand with pleasure. The well-remembered aroma of stale whisky floated round me.

'Aye, of course I do. I'd a knowed ye in a million, Miss Loulie. Heth, but ye're growed the big girl. A sight for sore eyes. Give me yer things.'

So I was Miss Loulie now. I handed him my rug.

'The porter has them,' I answered.

'That thief!' said Wattie, angry that I had wished to save him the burden.

'Miss Molly couldn't get away hersel',' he said, as he tucked the rug round my knees. 'She bid me tell ye she was sorry.'

'How is she? How's Bella and Theresa and poor grandfather?'

'We're all rightly, thank God, except the old Master. He's failed badly, Miss Loulie. It makes yer heart sore til see him look so badly and he not that old either.' My grandfather was over eighty years of age.

'I suppose Bella's just the same?'

'Oh, just the same. It'd take a strong wind to blow that one over.'

Aunt Molly was at the door to welcome me in. She kissed me and held me tight in her arms. It was so good to feel them about me once again.

Grandfather was not in bed as I had thought he

would be. He was sitting beside the fire, a glass of whisky by his side and his pipe in his hand. But he was not smoking. I noticed how terribly thin he had become, and how his hand shook when he stroked my hair. I could not speak at first.

'How are you, child?' he asked.

I nodded and smiled.

I took off my hat and coat and went into the kitchen to see Bella and to give myself a moment to recover from the sight of grandfather. Bella was standing at the fire, waiting for the kettle to boil. My tea was spread out on a tray. She looked as if I had only left her the day before.

'It's good to see you, daughter dear,' she said. 'I thought ye'd never come home again.'

'You've no notion how I wanted to.'

'I'll swear ye did. I'll wet yer tea now and bring it along in. Ye must be perished.'

Theresa gave me a wan smile and shook hands, but I could not be sure if any memory of me had lingered in her shadowy mind.

'What news is there of Justin?' I asked when I came back into the sitting-room.

'He'll be here to-morrow,' said Aunt Molly. 'But he can't stay long. He is expecting to be sent abroad shortly.'

I noticed that she did not say, 'to the Front'.

'What's he been doing? He never says much in his letters.'

'Well, you know he went to Oxford and intended

doing law. He did not seem very contented there. But, of course, everything has changed now. We don't know what will happen.'

'Tell me, Loulie,' asked grandfather, 'what are your plans?'

'I want to go to Dublin, Grandfather. I don't like the Lagan. The people there are so strange, so unfriendly. All during the Ulster Volunteer Movement they were horrible and they're as bad now about the war. I don't belong to them. I belong to you and I want to be with people like you. I hate their black self-righteous Protestant God.'

'Loulie dear,' said Aunt Molly, gently, 'don't be so harsh.'

'She's young yet,' grandfather smiled. 'What do you intend to do in Dublin?'

'I would like to go to College. I'm working for a Junior Exhibition. But even if I get it, I won't have enough to support myself. I might get some sort of a job in a school, something that would keep me while I studied.'

'What does your father say to that?'

'He doesn't say much, but mother does. I'm sure he wouldn't mind helping me if mother were willing. She says that because I have no brother I am not to imagine that I can claim the advantages he would have got. She says too that I will be spoiled for everything else — I suppose she means marriage. She doesn't approve of higher education for women.'

'She wouldn't,' grandfather chuckled.

He was in great spirits. I was beginning to forget he was so ill.

'I'll send you your clothes,' said Aunt Molly.

'Thank you, darling, you never forget me.'

'I'll have a great time fitting them on in the shops in Derry,' she laughed. 'The girls will think I've gone mad and am looking for a husband.'

'You are sweet.' I kissed her. 'Now tell me more about Justin.'

'He'll tell you himself when he comes. He's a poor letter writer. And somehow I think he's not at peace with himself. He never was, even as a little boy. Perhaps if he comes through safely he will settle down to life in earnest.'

It was strange how little there was to say, yet how happy we were in saying it. I played piquet with grandfather until it was time to go to bed.

That night I slept in the great four-poster bed in which Justin had slept. I lay awake for a long time, happy and content, not wishing to fall asleep, looking at the dark frame of the wool-work picture of Moses which hung over the mantelpiece and watching the shadows cast by the firelight on the walls. The old house had taken me back and I felt sheltered and protected within its walls. The rain pattered heavily on the window-panes.

I crept down under the blankets and fell asleep.

It was a strange Justin who arrived at the old house. He had grown tall and angular, his bony frame had not yet filled out, his cheeks were hard and lean, his eyes darkly sunk in their sockets. The depth of his voice surprised me. I noticed that at table he ate in an absent-minded way until there was no food left. He wandered from one room to another like an uneasy spirt. Aunt Molly looked anxiously at him from time to time, but grandfather seemed to take his restlessness for granted.

After lunch he wandered into the small study where I was reading and stood looking out of the window at the wide cobbled yard, swept by the rain. He turned round abruptly and said:

'Get your coat on, Lou, and come for a walk.'

'It's raining,' I replied. 'We'd get wet through.'

'Come on. You're not sugar, you won't melt.'

We went out, shivering at first in the gusty wind which blew in cold and hard from the sea. The mountains were covered with a rain mist which every now and then was torn apart, letting us see Slieve Snaght already covered with snow. We passed through the village and found it deserted. The geese lay huddled together in the lee of a grassy mound, their heads under their wings. The doors of the houses were shut tight against the weather and through the windows we could see the gleam of the turf fires. Everyone was indoors. We passed Aunt Anne's cottage, now closed and empty, no smoke rising from its chimney, for she had died two years previously.

We turned into the shore road. Here we met the full force of the gale which came tearing up the bay.

The water lay flat and grey under it and the scudding rack was grey and cold over our heads. The rain beat on our faces and the wind caught our breath so that we had to turn our heads sideways to breathe. Presently we took shelter behind a stone wall for a few minutes. Justin put his head close to mine.

'It's good to feel this wind, Loulie,' he said. 'God knows when we'll come here again.'

'Poor grandfather,' I sighed.

'Poor us. He's happy but we've got all our lives before us.'

'But that's what's grand, Justin. We've got it all before us. To do what we like with.'

'I wonder,' he said. 'More likely it will do what it likes with us.'

'Don't talk like that, it's silly. It's good to be alive.'

He smiled slowly, turning down one corner of his mouth.

'What a trite phrase, Lou. It's best to be like grandfather, contentedly facing the end, knowing there's nothing more the bastard can do to you.'

I looked hard at my cousin. His eyes were looking far away, through the mist.

'What's happened to you, Justin?'

He shrugged his shoulders.

'Nothing. Or nothing that hasn't happened to thousands of others and will happen to you and to millions more. Let's go on. What do you say to climbing Cranaigh?'

'In this weather?'

'All the better.'

'All right, boy, lead on.'

We turned from the shore road and took a path which led to the land side of the hill. Cranaigh rose abruptly from the sand dunes, just where the bay opened out into the sea. It would be next to impossible to try it on the side facing the sea. We struggled on. The rain poured down our faces, worked its way under the flaps of our coats and trickling down inside wetted us to the skin. We climbed on, gasping for breath. Once or twice I struck and, leaning against the sheltered side of a stone wall, refused to go any farther. Justin did not argue the point. He stood waiting for me to recover and then he led on. We got to the top and here the wind tore at our clothes forcing us down again. But as we turned back the wind tore the rack apart and for a few seconds we could see the sea boiling over the bar just below us and the great gloomy bens with their noses smothered in foam.

When we got down to the road again, I was so exhausted that I sat down on the wet road. Justin looked down at me.

'I'm sorry, my dear.'

'It's all right. I'll be better in a few minutes. It's a long time now since I've taken such violent exercise. Let's get home to the stable. Thank God Aunt Molly will give us some hot toddy and not hot currant tea and a bath as my mother would.'

'We're lucky to have known Aunt Molly, Lou. She helps us to forgive our families.'

That was the only time he said anything about his home. It must have been very little different from my own.

Aunt Molly did not send us to bed. As I had expected she made us some good hot punch and let us sit over the dining-room fire. The drink after the walk made us gay and talkative and Aunt Molly fussed around us like a nice hen. Justin became happy and lively. He sang scraps of popular songs which we had not heard, living as we did far away from music halls and concerts.

It was then that Aunt Molly told us why grandfather had sent for us. He wished to see us before he became so ill that he could not attend to business. He wanted to know what we wanted to do in life so that he could set aside some money for our use, which Aunt Molly would give us when we needed it. We were to be independent of our families. Justin's money would be kept for him until the end of the war.

'If I am killed, Aunt Molly,' he said, 'see that Loulie gets it. Mind what I am saying. I want it to go to Lou and to no one else.'

This was the only time we mentioned the possibility of Justin being killed. My knees shook and a strange ecstasy swept my mind.

'I'll see to that,' answered Aunt Molly.

'Thank you, my dear,' Justin stooped down and

kissed her. How small my pretty aunt had become.

We went into grandfather's sitting-room to say good-night. He brushed up his moustache in the same old way and kissed us affectionately on the cheek.

'Sleep well, children,' he said.

'Sleep well, grandfather,' we replied.

We took our candles and went up to bed side by side. The long dark corridors no longer seemed gloomy and sinister. Through the open doors of our bedrooms the firelight shone reflected in the dark polished wainscoting. The rain beat hard on the window-panes, making everything seem cosy and secure within.

I crept into the great four-poster bed and put out the candle. I was a little tipsy and the bed rose up round me, enveloping me. I lay watching the settling embers and thought pleasantly of the future. How pleasant it would be to get away from the North and live in Dublin. There I would find intellectual people, interested in painting and in writing. I would meet great men and women who had made their name in the world. I would see fine plays and hear good music. I would leave behind me for ever bigotry, fear and hatred. The door of a new world was open and my foot was on the threshold.

The door opened. It was Justin, tall and thin, looking more gaunt and bony than ever in his pyjamas. He was carrying his pillow in his hand.

'Can I come and talk to you?' he asked.

'Sure,' I answered.

'Then move yourself over and give me my half of the bed,' he said.

I moved over and he climbed in. He lay for a while without speaking or moving, his head thrown back on his arms. Then suddenly he turned to me and, burying his head on my shoulder, burst into tears.

'What's the matter?' I asked. 'Tell me, my dear, what's the matter?'

'The world, Lou, the world, it's a loathsome place.'

'We'll make it better, Justin,' I comforted him.

But that was all he said. He lay beside me, his head on my shoulder, his right arm thrown loosely round me.

I fell asleep. When I woke in the morning he was not there.

NEXT morning I stayed at home to help Aunt Molly paste covers on some jars and tidy up the store cupboard. Justin had gone for another long walk in the rain. I had refused to accompany him. In the cold light of day my pity for my cousin had ebbed and I felt rather irritated with him. He, on the contrary, seemed gay and cheerful as if he had shifted his burden of melancholy on to my shoulders.

'I don't know why I make so much jam and preserves,' said Aunt Molly briskly. 'We can't possibly get through it all. Every year I have to give away pounds and pounds of it. I must have a mean streak in me. I can't bear to see the fruit rot in the garden.'

'Keep it this time,' I answered. 'Mother is finding it difficult to get sugar already. Everyone is hoarding it.'

'How silly! The war will be over by Christmas.'

Bella opened the pantry door.

'There's a woman come,' she announced with obvious disapproval, 'asking for Mr. Justin. She calls herself Mrs. Thorauld.'

Aunt Molly looked very surprised and jumped down from the table on which she was standing.

'Mrs. Thorauld! Why didn't she let us know she was coming? Where is she?'

'In the small sitting-room, Miss Molly.'

Aunt Molly took off her apron, pushed her fingers through her curly hair and left the pantry hurriedly.

'Why on earth has Justin's mother come all this way?' I asked, as much to myself as to Bella.

'Thon's not his mother,' Bella remarked, setting her lips tightly.

'Who is it then?' I asked. My heart began to thump violently.

'God knows!' Bella remarked with pious disgust, and left me.

In a few minutes Aunt Molly was back.

'Loulie, Justin's wife has just arrived. I think you'd better come and help me talk to her.'

'Justin's wife! He's not married.'

'It appears that he is,' my Aunt answered gently. 'Please come — and be nice to her. She must find it very strange here.'

'What did he get married for?' I asked indignantly. 'He's too young to get married.'

'What does anyone get married for?' Aunt Molly was making an effort to deal with the situation and I was being difficult.

'Why does she come here?'

'Stop asking questions, Loulie. She's here and we must be nice to her. She probably needs all the kindness we can give her.'

Reluctantly, yet at the same time angry and curious, I followed Aunt Molly into the sitting-room. There, with her feet on the fender, her body bent over, her hands outstretched towards the fire, sat Justin's wife. Even to my jaundiced eyes she was extremely handsome. She was tall and rather thin. Her fair hair, wet with rain, clung in small tight curls to her forehead. She had rather prominent hazel eyes which lit up when she turned her head towards me and her white teeth glistened when she smiled. Aunt Molly introduced me:

'This is Loulie, Justin's cousin.'

I said nothing. I stood and stared at her, rudely and persistently. She stretched out a long thin hand.

'Pleased to meet the little cousin,' she said. 'My name's Nell, so don't stand on ceremony. It's sweet of you to be so nice to me. My heart was in my boots, I can tell you, as I tramped along the road. Thinks I to myself, if they throw me out on my ear at the end of this route march, I'm in the soup good and proper. Depressing road, isn't it?'

'You should have sent us word,' said Aunt Molly. 'We'd have met you at the station. Why on earth didn't you take a car?'

'Car? When I got out of that boneshaker that goes by the name of a train, all I could see was a donkey with spavins or rickets or whatever it is they get. My own legs looked better able to bear my weight.'

'I suppose your bag is at the station?'

'I left it in the charge of an elderly gentleman who wanted me to wait for the post car. He also told me that Glasthule was only a step.'

'You're wet through and you'll get your death of cold if we don't get you something to put on. I'll send Wattie to collect your bag and tell Bella to make a hot bath. I'm afraid neither my clothes nor Loulie's would fit you. Perhaps you had better put on Justin's pyjamas and dressing-gown and I'll see if Bella can find you a pair of slippers.'

My aunt was trying to relieve the tension by talking rapidly.

'You're awfully kind, you are really,' said Nell. 'I'm terribly ashamed of myself for dropping on you like this. I really had no idea.'

No idea of what, I thought. I had not opened my mouth. The anger that I felt against my cousin had momentarily transferred itself to his wife. Aunt Molly turned towards me and said sharply:

'Loulie, show Nell up to Justin's room and find his dressing-gown for her and some towels. I'll see to her bath and send Bella up with some tea.'

I rose and preceded Nell up the stairs, along the corridor to Justin's room. I still did not say anything. I knew I was behaving badly but this knowledge did not make me wish to behave any better. Nell stood at the foot of the bed, looking out dejectedly at the rain-drenched yard. I fetched Justin's dressing-gown and slippers, and some towels, and put a match to the fire.

'Queer place this,' Nell remarked as she approached the fire and began to undress.

'Do you think so?'

'Don't you? But I suppose you're used to it. As I came along the road, I ses to myself, Nell, my girl, you might have gone to the wilds of Borneo or the Frozen North when you were about it.'

'You must find it strange after London.' There was no cordiality in my tone.

'And how, dearie! To look at this place, you'd never think there was a war on. The last great adventure must have been the Flood.' She paused. 'And by the look of it we're in for another.'

'It doesn't rain all the time.'

'Glad to know it. I was beginning to get kind of nervous. Do you mean to say that Justin's out walking in this?'

'We don't mind it much.'

'I suppose it's all what you're used to.'

She struggled into the dressing-gown and went over towards the mirror. 'If there's one thing I hate, it's having my eyebrows washed down my face. I look like something washed up by the sea. No wonder you all looked surprised.'

Bella brought in a tray.

'Your bath will be ready soon, ma'am,' she announced acidly, and went out again.

'Who's she?' Nell asked, falling on the food.

'Bella. The cook. Please excuse me now. I hope you have everything you need.'

'Tooraloo,' Nell nodded cheerfully.

I found Aunt Molly in the kitchen, fussing around with the kettles.

'What does Justin mean . . . ?' I began, my anger boiling over.

'Loulie,' said Aunt Molly sharply, 'there are moments in our lives when we must behave well, if only for our own sakes. This is none of our business. If Justin is married, well then, he's married, and we must just accept it. Perhaps I hoped for something different, but I can't live Justin's life for him. Learn to bear with people. It can't be pleasant for that girl to find herself in this position, among strangers.'

'Then why did she come?'

'Justin's wife has a right to come.'

I had never before seen Aunt Molly so disturbed and irritated.

Half an hour later Nell came down, still in the dressing-gown. Aunt Molly brought her into grandfather's room and introduced her. But she did not stay long with him. She followed Aunt Molly back to the sitting-room. There was still no sign of Justin.

He returned in the middle of the afternoon. We could hear him in the hall. Then he opened the kitchen door and roared for his slippers. We did not hear Bella's answer but we heard Justin. With sharp, quick steps he walked the length of the hall, turned the handle and threw the door open with such force that it banged against the turf-box.

I was looking at Nell. She sat demurely examining the toast she held in her fingers, turning it over and nibbling at the corner. She made no move to go and meet Justin. She did not even look up when he entered the room.

'What the hell are you doing here?' he roared.

She looked up with a childishly surprised expression on her face.

'Eating toast. Very good toast, too. With plenty of butter on it.'

'Stop trying to be funny,' he shouted. 'What do you mean by coming here?'

'Justin,' said Aunt Molly. 'Do be quiet and sit down and have a cup of tea.'

'Yes, Justin,' said Nell. 'Do sit down. Nice welcome to give your loving wife who couldn't live another day without you.'

Justin's face went white and he was trembling with rage. He looked as if he could have murdered his wife. She paid not the slightest attention.

'I thought I told you to stay where you were,' his voice was low now and even. 'I left you all the money I had and told you to stay put. Understand? I won't have you or anyone else following me about.'

Here Aunt Molly got up and slipped out of the room beckoning me to follow. I stayed. Nothing could have dragged me away from that scene.

'I say, Justin,' Nell looked at him and grinned, a grin that made her face look roguishly attractive. 'I'm sorry but somehow or other, you know how it is, but I ran short of money. And I knew you wouldn't like me to ask Will Horner or any of the boys for it. I know how particular you are.'

'Particular, Hell! You couldn't have got through the money in twenty-four hours.'

'Boy, you don't know little Nell, she had her boots on when . . .'

'Shut up, you strap!' Justin banged the back of the chair with his fist. I went cold with horror and was glad that Aunt Molly was out of the room, glad, too, that Nell could not possibly have understood that word. She grasped its implication, however.

'Little gentleman!' she murmured.

I was amazed at her coolness and self-control. Why did she make no effort to defend herself against my cousin's attack?

'Oh, come off it, Justin. Keep your hair on. There's nothing to be afraid of. They like me here. They're awfully nice to me.'

Justin stood looking at his wife, making an effort to control himself.

'I'm sure they are,' he replied coldly. 'They'd be nice to anything I'd bring in. But that's no reason why they should be imposed on. Now, Nell, either you go or I go. Which shall it be?'

'I'm doing very nicely where I am, thank you. There, Justin, lay off it, like a good fellow. We're all friends here. Go out and get yourself a drink and cheer up.'

Justin turned on his heel and left the room. I expected her to follow him but she went on drinking her tea, as if a scene like this were quite in the order of the day. When she had drained her cup she put it down and remarked:

'Now, who'd have thought he'd carry on like that? Aren't men funny, dearie?'

'I suppose so,' I answered, thinking at the time that she must have known that Justin would be furious with her.

I was surprised myself when, ten minutes later, I heard Justin call me from the hall. I found him standing there, his bag at his feet, his wet coat over his shoulders.

'Good-bye, Lou,' he said in a gentle voice, placing his hand on my shoulder.

'You're not going, Justin?' I felt weak with grief.

'I'm going, dear. I've seen Aunt Molly and grandfather. But before I go I want to say one thing.' He paused. I felt my knees weaken. I almost prayed that he would offer no explanation. 'If I don't come back, what I said yesterday about the money holds good. Nell gets a pension, so she's all right. You're to have the cash. I'll go back through Dublin and see a lawyer there and make it all shipshape. Have my bag sent on to this address. Good-bye, sweet, good luck.'

I stood in the road in the driving rain and watched him walk down the village, past the forge. He walked on steadily, never looking back.

My cousin Justin had gone to the wars.

For one reason or another we all became very attached to Nell. Her continual good humour, her gaiety, her irresponsibility charmed everyone around her. In a couple of days we had forgotten her vulgarity, her speech, her cheap finery. Even Bella succumbed. Nell never forgot to thank her for the dinner, to compliment her on her baking and to ask humbly for special dishes.

Wattie made no attempt to resist her charms. The day after Nell's arrival he scandalized Bella by appearing in a clean shirt and collar, his Sunday tie and best suit. He suddenly began to look years younger. He shaved every day. He took to standing around in conspicuous places so that Nell should notice him.

Bella's scorn for his infatuation was tremendous.

'Look at the old goat,' she remarked to me. 'Skipping around like a lamb in the spring, with his chin shaved and his quiff oiled instead of making his peace with the Almighty. At his age it's his immortal soul he should be worrying about and not a young woman. And he old enough to be her granddaddy.'

Every time Bella found him hanging around, she found something for him to do, some particularly foul and dirty job which necessitated changing his suit. With the meekness of a martyr he would obey, paying no attention to Bella's heavy sarcasm, and then change back. Nothing could quell his ardour.

He even dragged down Justin's old saddle from its place in the loft and offered to teach Nell to ride. The lessons were a failure, but a source of deep joy to Wattie. Nell had a way of losing her head when she found herself perched high on the old cob's back. She would scream, throw herself off and Wattie would catch her. This was his greatest happiness. He bought violet cachous in the village shop to make his breath smell sweet. The effect when he opened his mouth was horrible.

She was good-natured and obliging and really liked busying herself with small tasks. When he was not too tired, she would play cards with grandfather for hours and entertain him hugely with stories about 'her old man' who ran a small public house somewhere in East Ham and who had apparently in a moment of outraged self-respect shown her the door. She fed the hens, standing in the yard in her high-heeled shoes, calling 'chuck-chuck' and laughing at their spiteful ways. She even tried to milk a cow. But I could never get her to go for walks. Her feet in their ridiculous shoes gave out after a mile or so. The wildness of the countryside and its poverty horrified her. Accustomed though she was to much more sordid poverty in a large city, she was frightened when she saw it in such a forbidding setting. She had never been nearer the country than Margate or Brighton.

After a few days one could see that she was beginning to weary of her quiet existence. She never read, not even the newspapers. She could not sew or cook or amuse herself in any way. Her abundant energies could find no outlet in my aunt's well-ordered household.

'Doesn't anything ever happen here?' she asked me some days after her arrival. She was lying on the sofa, gazing idly around the room. I was working at the table.

'Sometimes. A wedding, a birth, a funeral. Someone goes to America. Someone comes back.'

'What do you do when you want to amuse yourself?'

'Go for a walk. Go to see someone. Read a book. This is a quiet place.'

'So is the cemetery. Isn't there a pub here?'

'Three.'

'Why don't we go there?'

I was surprised that such an idea could occur to anyone.

'Women don't go to pubs in Ireland.'

'God, what sort of women are they? If there's anything I hate it's solitary drinking.'

'They don't drink.'

'Go on. Don't you ever?'

'If I'm out to dinner and then only a glass of wine.'

'What a life! It wouldn't do for little Nell. She's glad she was born a happy English child with a mug of beer in her hand. Not afraid to kick up her petticoats either. Nothing I like better than to get tight and have a bit. Don't you?'

I had not the slightest idea what she meant. But I was too polite or too shy to say so. I replied:

'Yes, of course.'

'You bet,' she said with that grin which made her face so attractive. 'Nothing to come up to it. You and Justin must have had some fine times together.'

'Of course,' I repeated.

'Justin's a great lad when you get him going. Only trouble with him is he's got too many moods. He's apt to come to pieces in your hand, like the china vase. And doesn't he get gloomy, like my old man when he'd backed some old hair trunk that forgot it ought to be trying? Now when I get like that, I just mosey off to a pub and tank up. Nothing like it for throwing the old black dog off your back. Then if you've any luck you can pick up some fellow and have a good blow-out. Nothing like it. That's what I tell Justin.'

The drift of this conversation was becoming plain to my untutored ears.

'But surely, Nell, you love Justin.'

'Love Justin?' She looked at me as if the idea had only just occurred to her. 'Oh, he's all right. Good fun when he gets going. But the worst of him is he's so moody.'

I forced myself to go on with the subject. I wanted to find something out.

'I'm sure he loves you,' I said.

Nell laughed, a gay, light-hearted laugh.

'Does he? I don't know. I don't think he loves anyone. He's just sorry for them. Sorry for himself, too. It's only when you're miserable he really likes you. Do you know,' she paused to give emphasis to the words, 'He's even sorry for me. Wants to save me from myself. I'd sooner he hit me in the face. But I don't stand it for long. I clear out and when I get back I don't give a continental who's sorry for me. I'm past it.'

I began to see what Justin's life must have been like. I said nothing to Aunt Molly but I am sure she knew. There was very little about her children which Aunt Molly did not know.

'How did you get to know Justin?' I asked.

'I'm not very clear about the introduction, dearie. There's very little about that evening that remains in my mind. I think it was in one of the pubs near Tottenham Court Road. There's a lot of pubs round there. I was stringing along with Bill Horner just then. Poor Bill, he wasn't half a bad sort when you knew him. He could be awf'ly good fun. One time the two of us . . .'

I brought her back to the subject.

'That was the night you met Justin?'

'Oh yes, Bill had an awful jag on that night. He was annoyed about something or other and I must have got his goat with something I said. Not that I meant it, you know. I often say things just to relieve my feelings. So Bill gave me one just to relieve his.

That's the worst of men, you know, dearie, they're so moody. When I came to I was rolling along in a taxi with a perfect stranger. He asked me where I lived. When I was getting out, I said to him, "Aren't you coming up?" and he followed me in.'

'And then?'

'He did seem a bit astonished when I threw Bill's pyjamas at him. The next morning I was in an awful way. You know, dearie, if I'm not careful about my drinks I get like that. He sent for a doctor and told him that I was his wife. The doctor looked at us and shook his head. But then, he'd seen some queer sights.'

'Did Justin go on living with you?'

'For a few days and then he had to go. Leave was up. Before he went we got married. He said he was sure that he'd be killed and he wanted to leave me something, if it was only a pension from a grateful country. It's queer now, all the other fellows I knew, not one of them thought he'd be killed, he always thought it would be the other fellow.'

Nell was not one to remain long without diversion. She began an ardent flirtation with a young clergyman who had just come to the parish. For a week he called every day to inquire about grandfather and take Nell for a walk. Then realizing where Nell's attentions were undoubtedly leading him, he sheered off. Nell bore him no grudge, nor did she, as a country girl would have done, follow him about. She just let him slip from her mind.

It was when she was on an errand for Aunt Molly to the village shop that she met Tom O'Donnell. He was the son of a woman, locally known as Black Sally, who kept a fishing inn some miles away. He had just got a commission in the army and was home on leave. He had a ramshackle car which he drove up and down to Derry and he had the reputation of being a wild lad when his mother was not taking care of him.

That afternoon Nell rolled up to the house in Tom's car. He was rather loath to come in, but Aunt Molly went out and invited him in. He was ill at ease and sat on the edge of his chair, looking very miserable and dejected. Nell was in great form. She laughed and joked and it was plain to be seen that she was a little drunk.

'I say, Tom,' she said. 'How long would it take us to get to Derry?'

'About an hour and a half.'

'Put your foot on the gas and make it an hour. Come along, Lou, we'll go up and have a good time.'

I caught Aunt Molly's eye and declined. I went back to my books and Aunt Molly to her sewing.

'Aunt Molly,' I asked, 'why do people drink?'

Aunt Molly looked up and replied dryly:

'Your grandfather says it is because of some secret sorrow of the soul.'

Two days later Nell turned up in a bedraggled condition. She looked as if she had slept in her clothes and had not been very particular where she had slept. She was very black under the eyes and shook as if she were cold. She was one of those women who are vociferous in their misery. She burst into tears, called herself foul names and wished she were dead. She moaned and cursed in a way which must have horrified my poor aunt. But if she was shocked Aunt Molly did not show it. She hustled Nell up to bed, made her hot coffee and ordered Bella to put a couple of hot water bottles in the bed. Still moaning as if in great pain, physical and mental, Nell fell asleep, and slept the clock round. When she came downstairs she was as bright as a button and as unrepentant as a fallen angel. She laughed at our long faces and remarked:

'I always do say that there's nothing does you so much good as a blow-out.'

'Perhaps so,' answered Aunt Molly. 'But nothing will do you so much good at this moment, my girl, as a good meal.'

'Lead me to it,' Nell answered with a grin.

After that she was quiet for a day or two. Then the old restlessness began to return. She disappeared again with Tom O'Donnell who apparently could not keep away from her. My aunt seemed to accept all this as perfectly natural. At least she said nothing to me.

The affair soon became the talk of the country-side. Nell spent more of her time in Tom O'Donnell's car than she did at home. They could be seen tearing along the roads in every stage of insobriety. Then

Tom O'Donnell's mother, a woman of purpose and power, a woman with a strong right arm, took matters into her hands and gave Tom a good horse-whipping. The news spread far and wide as it has a way of doing in the country and I am afraid no one was more amused and delighted than Nell. The whipping seemed to cool his ardour and for a few days Nell hung about the house, bored and weary. I am sure that if she had had the money she would have gone. But Justin had not sent her any and she did not like to borrow from Aunt Molly. Then Tom O'Donnell's leave was up and she went with him.

She wrote to me later from London. How she managed to get back there was a mystery to me at the time. I know better now.

She said nothing about Justin in her letter. As he wasn't there at the time, he did not mean anything to her. It was good to be back in London and everything was fine. I ought to take her advice and throw those old books of mine in the fire and come over to her. She'd show me what life was like.

I had a short note from Justin.

'It's good-bye, for a while anyway. I'm leaving to-day. The name of my solicitor is Finnigan, address 8 Upper Ormond Street. Keep your heart up.'

I was sitting over my books, not really working, just turning the pages and thinking of Nell, when the door opened and Aunt Molly came into the room.

'Loulie, there's a visitor for you in the kitchen.' She smiled as she looked down at me.

'For me? In the kitchen?'

'He wouldn't come in here.'

A tall young man, in the uniform of a private soldier, was standing with his back to the kitchen window. I did not recognize him at first. I took his hand and stood looking at him.

'You don't remember me?' His blue eyes, eyes as cold and glittering as the sea, smiled at me.

'I'm sorry.'

I looked at him more closely.

'Egan O'Doherty!' I exclaimed.

'Aye,' said Bella, rapping the edge of a saucepan with her potstick. 'Egan O'Doherty it is. And more shame to him to be seen in that coat.'

'It is the same coat as my cousin wears,' I answered sharply.

'It's one thing for the young master til wear it, but it's a mortal disgrace til see it on the back of his father's son.'

Egan paid no attention to this outburst.

'I've brought you a present from my mother,' he

said to me. 'Just to welcome you home. She'd have come herself but she thought maybe you'd rather see me.'

There was an impudent smile on his face and his eyes danced with merriment as he handed me the parcel. It contained a hand-knit jersey, such as I had worn as a child, a fat chicken and a dozen duck eggs.

'How did she remember I liked duck eggs?'

'I remembered.'

'Thank her kindly for me and tell her I'll come along and thank her myself.'

'Come to-night.'

'Why to-night?'

He picked up his cap from the table and held out his hand again.

'Good-bye till to-night, then,' he answered, and left.

'Bella,' I said furiously. 'Have you no manners?'

'I keep them for them as deserves them,' she answered, and taking me by the shoulders pushed me out of the kitchen.

The O'Doherty's had a small farm outside the village. When I entered the kitchen that evening, Mrs. O'Doherty was seated in a high chair by the fire, knitting. She was a powerful woman, tall and broad-shouldered. She ruled her family and all those about her like a despot. No one, least of all her husband, questioned her will. As I came through the door, I noticed how handsome and majestic she looked. The firelight shone on her fair hair, as fine and glistening as that of a young girl. It was brushed straight back from her high forehead and gathered in a bag at the back of her neck. Her face was lean and high-coloured with prominent cheek-bones. Her hands, hardened with work, were firm and lean. The needles flickered in the light, to and fro, with a sharp clicking sound. She rose as I closed the door behind me. I glanced round the room. There was no sign of Egan.

'Draw up to the fire, daughter,' she cried. Her voice was harsh and high, a voice often thrust against the wind. Egan's father, a tall, thin, silent man, brought a stool and set it close to the fire.

'Thank you for the jersey, Mrs. O'Doherty,' I said. 'It was very kind of you to think of it and to take all that trouble.'

'Don't talk about it, child. Hanna and I can knit a jersey in a couple of evenings. It will serve to keep you warm in the cold days. We're glad to see you back amongst us. How is your granddad?'

'He's not so well to-day. We don't expect him to last long now. But you never can tell. He's up one day and down the next.'

'The strong die hard.'

The kettle was put on the fire and while it was coming to the boil I was told everything that had happened to the family while I had been away. Mary was a school-teacher. Hugh worked on the farm. Manus had gone to America. Hanna, a tall,

117

delicate girl with her mother's beautiful fair hair, and bright blue eyes, was helping at home. It was said in the village that she had consumption.

'Egan, God help us, stopped right in his second year at the university to go to the war. It's a great pity.' No word of complaint, yet it must have been a great blow to them. To send a son to the university cost untold sacrifice in a family like this, even if he had a scholarship. 'He's very clever,' his mother went on with pride. 'It's a great pity, indeed, to interrupt his studies when he was getting on so well. But we mustn't grumble. We must pray God to send him back safe to us.'

I knew that good manners demanded that I should now tell my story. I told them about my home in the Lagan, my school, my plans. Mrs. O'Doherty nodded with approval. She liked young people to work and get on. She had the reputation of being an ambitious, crafty but good-hearted woman.

Not a word was said on either side about Justin. The scandal of his marriage had spread and it was felt to be good manners not to discuss the matter. After I had drunk some tea and chatted about the weather and the crops and the financial state of the country, I rose to go. Hanna offered to come with me. I refused with a laugh. As if I couldn't find my way home in my own country.

As I stood in the yard, a dark figure came from one of the barns and joined me. It was Egan. He took my hand gently in his to help me down the stony lane where the deep cart ruts were filled with water. At the age of seventeen the touch of a young man's hand has an intimacy which in later life no other contact can ever have. My hand trembled in his.

Cold moonlight lay like a thin sheet over everything and when we came out on the road that led to the village, the bay lay below us like a pool of steel with the mountains behind, black except where the light caught the first snow. This is my home, I thought, only here can I feel peaceful and happy. There can be nowhere in the world so beautiful. The fear of the future lay heavy on me and I clung to this familiar place.

'When are you leaving?' I asked Egan.

'The morrow. This is my last leave.'

'Aren't you sorry?'

'I don't know,' he answered slowly. 'I'm never sorry to be doing something, going places.'

'I shall be leaving here in a day or two. I shall be sorry.'

'Are you going to Dublin?'

'Next autumn.'

'I'll see you there, maybe. Don't forget me.'

We came to the gate.

'Won't you come in?' I asked.

'No, thank you.' He stood beside me tall and dark. His head looked finely drawn and cold in the moonlight and his eyes glittered under their heavy brows. I put my hand on the latch and again it met his. Here in the moonlight I felt afraid of this strange young man.

'Before I go . . .' He did not finish the sentence. His arm slipped round my shoulders and held me fast. His head bent over mine and he kissed me. I flung the door of the gate open and rushed through the yard, like any frightened girl. I heard him laugh as he closed the gate behind me.

Two days later I left for the Lagan. It was easier than I thought to say good-bye to grandfather. He brushed up his moustache and kissed me as if we were saying good-night.

'Good-bye, child. Take care of yourself and don't work too hard.'

At the station Wattie almost wept. Since Nell's departure he had sunk again to his old man's estate.

'Come back,' he cried out after me. 'Come back soon.'

WHEN I arrived back in the Lagan, the war fever had reached its height. Everyone who was not taking part in some war work or other was branded pro-German. This did not mean that the suspects were ostracized. On the contrary they were visited frequently and questioned delicately as to what they thought of the war. Reports of statements they made or were supposed to have made were forwarded to the authorities. As a rule these communications were anonymous. The District Inspector of Police, a young Scotsman called McKenzie, who was waiting for his commission to be transferred to the army, confided to my father that 'the old women of this place, male and female, were driving him daft'.

Scattered over the country were German craftsmen, draftsmen and skilled dyers. Many of them had married Irishwomen but had never troubled to become naturalized. Such things did not trouble people before the war. They were spied on, watched day and night, treated like lepers, frequently dismissed. All sorts of allegations were made against them. They were taking photographs, they were signalling aeroplanes, they were sending code messages by carrier pigeons. That there were no fortifications to photograph, no aeroplanes to signal, did not matter in the least. No matter how ridiculous these stories were, they were believed. My father fell under suspicion for trying to defend these unfortunate men. He and McKenzie did what they could to laugh down this hysteria, but with no success. One by one the Germans were taken off, and their wives were left with little or no money to struggle through the war years, at enmity with their neighbours and forbidden by the law to travel more than five miles from their homes.

The spy scare died down as suddenly as it had sprung up. The first lists of dead and wounded began to come in. Whole companies were wiped out. Many of those boys who had gone forth so bravely would never return and more were asked to fill the gaps. Boys scarcely free from school were joining the army. The women began to go about with grey faces and eyes full of fear. In their hearts they hated those women whose sons had escaped or were safe in hospital, perhaps crippled for life, and most of all they hated those women who had no sons. They began to shout for conscription. They sent white feathers, wrote letters and talked hysterically. Let every man be taken.

But underneath all this there was a current of disillusion. Here and there people began to say that it had always been like this. The Irish boys were being sacrificed. This is England's war, not ours, some said, but quietly. Others said, if all our lads are killed who will defend us from the Catholics? Stories of the Boer War, of the needless sacrifice of Irish soldiers were told in the farm-houses in the evening when work was over. The word 'Spion Kop' was heard again, spoken aloud in the street by hard-lipped men. One man, more bigot and more courageous than the rest, asked in public why our men should die fighting against 'Protestant Germany for Catholic Belgium and Infidel France'. After the disaster of Gallipoli no more men went.

Grandfather died in February. My father and mother went north and my father returned immediately after the funeral. I found him quite pleasant to live with when my mother was not there. In the evening he talked to me of many things, of the war, of politics, of my future. In that short week I came to know him better, to appreciate the just balance of his mind. One evening our neighbour Mr. Edgington and the District Inspector McKenzie dropped in. McKenzie had come to say good-bye. He was leaving the following week. There was the usual talk about the progress of the war. Edgington was optimistic. McKenzie thought England was beaten or as good as beaten. She would never emerge from this conflict whole. Presently my father asked:

'McKenzie, what is the law about the only son of a widow?'

'He can be sent home if his mother asks for him. Why?'

'An old woman came to see me to-day. Her only son worked for me before he joined the army. She is destitute, or nearly so, and she came to ask me if I could do anything for her.'

'Tell her to come and see me. If it's the last act I do in an official capacity, I'll save one man from the shambles.'

'Who will you put in his place?' Edgington demanded.

'Myself,' answered McKenzie.

Edgington looked at him with some disgust.

'If I didn't know that you had volunteered, McKenzie, I'd look on you as a pro-German.'

McKenzie's rude Scotch face went a trifle redder.

'You can look on me as any bloody thing you like, Edgington,' he replied. 'I'm going into this war with my eyes open and not because I believe in it. I just feel that I can't stay safe at home when other men are being killed. I've neither animosity nor enthusiasm. Don't think it's any pleasure to me to fight and get killed to bring you and your like fat profits.'

'We're running short of labour,' said my father. 'High wages will eat up our profits.'

'Put the lassies on the machines,' shouted McKenzie. 'Lassies and old men. But for God's sake, man, keep the flag of profit flying.'

They wrangled and fought all evening.

'This is a just war, a holy war, a war against aggression,' shouted old Edgington.

McKenzie burst into howls of laughter, slapped his knees and laughed again. There was mockery and bitterness in his laughter.

'The rights of small nations!' he barked. 'The

biggest robber nation in the world fights for the rights of small nations. Always provided they are somebody else's small nations.'

'You can't deny it,' shouted Edgington.

'I can and will. What do you say, Delahaie? Don't you think this small nation business is the rankest hypocrisy?'

'To tell you the truth,' said my father, 'I agree with you. I think that if it had suited England to invade Belgium herself, she'd have done it — but with this difference, she'd have done it more cleverly, she would not have appeared to have done it. I don't underrate the cleverness of the English.'

'Didn't I tell you?' McKenzie slapped my father on the back. 'You're the only honest man I know. Make your profits, man. I don't grudge you them.'

'I won't make much,' said my father smiling. 'I manufacture linen, not munitions.'

'If I didn't know you, if I didn't know you were really a brave man, I'd think you a coward,' said Edgington fiercely.

'But I am a coward,' McKenzie grinned with the simple malice of his kind. 'That's why I'm going. I'm joining the herd instead of going to jail as an anti-war propagandist. Do you think I'm proud of myself? If ever a son of mine says, "What did you do in the Great War, Daddy?" I'll squirm, because I'll have to say, "I did what the others did, son, I murdered my fellow-men".'

'How dare you talk like that to me?' Edgington's voice was shrill with anger, 'to me, who has given my two sons.'

'I hope you remember that some day,' McKenzie answered, rising to go.

In the hall he apologized to my father.

'I'm sorry I was so thran with the old man,' he said. 'We're the devil for arguing, we Scots.'

'Well, good luck to you. Come back safe to us.'

'I'll do my best.' Then he turned to me and took both my hands in his.

'Good-bye, lass. I'm sorry for ye. All your young men have been taken away.'

When we returned to the drawing-room old Edgington had calmed down.

'His heart's in the right place, I'm sure it is,' he said pathetically. 'He wouldn't be going if his heart wasn't right.'

'He's a bad-tempered Scotsman,' my father soothed him. 'He only means half he says.'

'Maybe you're right,' muttered the old man. 'Maybe you're right.'

When my mother returned, she returned in a royal rage. So deep was her sense of injustice that she would scarcely speak to me. Her acidulous asides and involved hints drove my father into one of his tempers. She clung, like a queen of drama, to my two young sisters. They, poor children, were at a loss to understand the cause of this domestic upheaval. Though more accustomed to my mother's dramatic moments than I was, they were seldom personally involved.

She had quarrelled with my aunt. That in itself was nothing new. But it appeared from barbed remarks let drop at table that I was responsible in some way for the rupture. Except at meals my mother did not address me at all, except through a third person. At table one morning, when my father was beginning to recover his good humour, she demanded that he should write a stiff letter to my aunt and see his lawyer. My father answered sharply:

'See MacIntyre? What about?'

'About the will, of course. No one could suppose for a moment that Molly has not been exercising undue influence. After all, he was my own father and he didn't leave me a penny. Something peculiar in that. Everything goes to Molly and her two darlings. Why should I be passed over for my own daughter? Why should Molly be given charge of the money as if the child's parents were not to be trusted. I knew she was hatching some plot when she sent for Loulie. I'll break that will if it's the last thing I do.'

'Your father knew you were provided for,' my father answered with sharp emphasis. 'You got a definite share in the business and I bought out your brother. What more do you want?'

'She would not let me near him when he was ill. I know he always loved me. She probably told him

I would not come. A thousand pounds for Loulie and another for that good-for-nothing boy, Justin Thorauld. It's disgraceful. And the house is to be theirs, too. Molly would not let me take one stick out of it, not as much as one of my mother's sheets. I call it unjust.'

By this time my father had completely lost control of his temper.

'This is my last word,' he shouted. 'Don't draw me into your family quarrels. You nearly landed me into a lawsuit with your brother once. I've got enough troubles on my shoulders already. I don't care who gives Loulie money. Let her take it and do what she likes with it, only leave me alone. I don't give a damn who inherits that house. I don't want to live in it. There's far too much furniture in this house already. And mark what I say, you're going to no lawyer about this.'

He flung his chair against the table and marched out.

My mother looked at me with anger. Then a self-satisfied smile distorted her features, a smile which I hated.

'You'll have your way,' she said. 'Thanks to your aunt and her machinations. But remember no one has ever prospered without a mother's blessing. Come, children.' This was addressed to my sisters. 'I want you to help your mother sort the linen.'

That spring and the following summer I worked all day. I did not go to school except for special classes. My father let me work in his study and often in the evenings he would spend an hour or two with me, helping me with my Latin and mathematics. He seemed to like me these days. I asked once or twice if I could go and stay with Aunt Molly, but was always refused. My mother did not write to my aunt so I must not visit her.

In the autumn I went up to Dublin and entered the University with an exhibition. Aunt Molly wrote to me and sent me the money I needed.

For some months after my entrance into the university I did little or no work. I attended lectures, but the rest of the day I spent exploring the old streets, looking at the old houses and squares, meandering along the quays. I wandered through Phoenix Park and climbed the Dublin Hills. It became one of my chief delights to lie up there and watch the great plain, the Plain of the Birds, stretching far away to the Gap of the North, and west to Galway Town. I thought of Red Hugh, the last of the Irish Chieftains, wandering through these hills, cold and frost-bitten, after his escape from Dublin Castle. I remembered how at last he had turned his face north again making for his own mountains in Donegal. I used to follow his path through the mountains, knowing that from that day to this nothing had changed of what I saw around me.

I found the lazy life of Dublin soothing after the harshness of the North, and the indifference of the people charming. No one troubled about me, no one inquired what I was doing, or why I did no work. If I did not attend lectures, I would lose my term, that was all. The examinations were a long way off and did not trouble me. I did not worry about anything, my work, my future, the human beings around me. I went on like this till Easter.

I was at home in the Lagan at the time of the Easter Week Rising. All the old fear and hatred of the Catholics broke out again. English soldiers were drafted into the town and two of the officers were billeted on us. They were gay young men who had not yet seen active service and were rather surprised to find themselves in Ireland and not in France. When the Rising had been put down and the leaders shot, the atmosphere of smug satisfaction among the Unionists was so horrible that I only thought of getting away. I asked my father to find out if I could get back to Dublin, giving as excuse that I wanted to read in the library, being unable to get German text-books during the war. The presence of the young officers in the house made him consent, particularly as one of them, in a clumsy, boyish way, had begun to make love to me. I went south in the first train to cross the Donabate Viaduct.

Dublin was still smouldering when I entered it. O'Connell Street lay in ruins. Everywhere there was the rank smell of burning and stale ashes. Even through the rain the smoke still rose from some of the buildings. Companies of soldiers marched through the streets and groups stood here and there on guard. Most of the shops were still closed. The city was in mourning.

A feeling of horror and dread took hold of me. The war had caught us up.

I saw that beneath the casual indifference of these people, beneath their quiet good humour, there was an inflexible spirit. There must be something to bring about this upheaval, to rouse a small group of men against the mightiest power on earth. The talk of German gold was so much nonsense that took in no one, not even those who professed to believe. I began to buy revolutionary newspapers and pamphlets. I became interested in the work and writings of James Connolly, and I was not the only one. Small groups began to spring up simultaneously. Books were passed around and read. Arguments—bitter, immature arguments—broke out among the students in the club, which often ended in reviling and personal abuse. Meanwhile the war went on. The lists of dead and wounded continued to come in.

It was my professor who brought me back to my senses. He sent for me. I went along to his rooms, wondering what was in store for me. He gave me a cup of tea and talked of those things which were at the moment of greatest importance to me, politics and religion, but in a more universal way than I had yet heard them discussed. Only when I rose to go did he mention my work. He said that he had noticed that I had been doing no work. That wasn't a bad thing sometimes, but I needn't make a habit of it. There was a lot to learn and most of it was quite pleasant. Would I care to attend some special lectures he was giving for those intending to present themselves for the Scholarship examinations? I need not go up for the examination but I might find the lectures amusing. I went back to my books.

I seldom went home, and then only for a few days.

I always said that I had to read in the library. I would have gone to see Aunt Molly, but suddenly I got a letter from her telling me that she was married. It had never occurred to me that my aunt was still young enough to get married.

'. . . I was married quietly last week to Dr. Rice, who has been staying here, fishing. I am not sorry to leave my old home for it is sad now and empty. Your new uncle is a widower with two small children. Isn't it nice to think I have a family all ready made for me, a boy and a girl whom no one can take away from me?

'If you and Justin do not mind, and I'm sure you won't, we would like to come back here sometimes for a holiday. It will be pleasant to hear the laughter of children again in the old home.

'You know, I suppose, that by your grandfather's will you inherit one hundred and fifty pounds a year if I marry, and the remainder of my income when I die. This does not come into force until you are twenty-one, but if you want the money now, do tell me. I have plenty, and I am not marrying a poor man.

'You and Justin will have to keep up the old house now. Let me know if I can make any arrangements for you. I suppose you have heard that Justin has been wounded and is in hospital in Malta. . . .'

I wrote to Justin. The reply came a fortnight later.

'I'm getting well again. I'm glad to hear of Aunt Molly's marriage. Make what arrangements you like about the house, but don't sell it while I am alive. If Bella's still there, get her to look after it. She won't get married. She's had all the fun she ever wanted out of bullying Wattie. Go and see Finnigan and make arrangements. This place is awful, all white and staring. I long for green fields again and soft rain. All the best.

'Your loving cousin,
Justin.'

I went to see Justin's lawyer and agreed to pay seventy pounds a year towards the upkeep of the house and Bella's wages. Justin could contribute a similar sum. If more was needed, Finnigan could let us know. I heard no more for years from my cousin Justin.

Just before the final examinations I went to see my professor again. I asked him what I should do when I left. He lifted one eyebrow and looked at me with an amused smile.

'Now, how should I know? I live a life as sheltered as that of a nun. What do you want to do?'

'I've been offered a job at my old school. But I would hate living there and I hate the very thought of teaching.'

'You'd be a damned bad teacher.'

'I know. But what would I be damned good at?'

'Only at something you really liked. What do you like?'

'I want to work on a newspaper. How do I go about it? Do I write articles and send them in?'

'I am a child in the ways of the world,' he said in his light satirical voice. 'But I do know that's not the way. The editors have all sorts of little printed labels. They just attach one to the front page and send it back. The office boy can usually be trusted to do that.'

'Do you know anyone on a paper?'

'Not the kind who would be the slightest use to you, child. But I've noticed that men, as a rule, find it hard to say "No". They'll say "Call again" or "Perhaps something may turn up later". They'll never say "No" unless irritation or anger gives them courage. Remember the parable of the importunate widow.'

'What do you think I should do?'

'Make the rounds of all the papers and then begin all over again. In the end someone will say "Yes". Have you any money?'

'My scholarship money and some my grandfather left me. Enough.'

'Don't tell anyone,' said the professor laughing. 'Or you'll have the fortune hunters after you.'

THAT was how I met Tom Hennessy. I had been dragging round the newspaper offices for weeks without seeing anyone of importance. Then one afternoon I drifted into the offices of the *Evening Recorder*, a dirty ramshackle building behind the Theatre Royal. The entrance hall smelled of old boots and cats and the farther one penetrated the more varied and mixed were the smells. It was quite impossible to see the editor. To judge from the guileless countenance of the young man at the desk it was doubtful if there was an editor or, if there was, no one had seen him for so long that the police ought to have been informed. The paper seemed to come out without any directing hand.

I was listening with a pleasant smile on my face and rage in my heart to the long preamble of the mild-mannered and guileless clerk when someone touched me on the shoulder. I turned round and found myself facing a tall bony man of about thirty-five years of age. He was dressed in a rather dirty trench-coat and wore a soft hat pulled down over his eyes. He had a long reddish face and his thin mouth curved down when he smiled. He was smiling now.

'Anything I can do for you, lady?' he asked in a strong western accent.

'You can tell me when the editor, if there is one,

is likely to come out of his coma and be able to see me.'

'The editor, fair lady, is in no coma. He drinks nothing stronger than soda water, or cocoa when he feels like being one of the boys. But he might pass into one if you were to see him at this moment.'

'Why?'

'He's a sensitive plant. When he sees the light of battle in a female eye — even in a beautiful female eye — he folds up his petals and rings for his secretary. Ever seen his secretary? No? She's the original model of the bearded lady and she takes wonderful care of our editor. I don't know what his wife would do without her. Now what do you want to see him about? Is it about one of the leading articles, because if it is he didn't write it, I did.'

'I want a job,' I said weakly.

'You *want* a job. Well, there's no accounting for tastes. Still, come along and talk to me about it. We'll have some tea. I'm near dead for the want of it.'

'What's your name?' he asked over the tea-table.

'Anne-Louise Delahaie.'

'God in Heaven, what a mouthful. What are you called in more intimate moments?'

'Loulie or Lou.'

'That'll do fine. Mine's Tom Hennessy. Now what gave you the idea of being a newspaper woman? You know only women of canonical age are eligible. It wouldn't be good for the boys.'

'I want to work on a newspaper.'

'You do. Here, Jenny.' The waitress came forward, gave the table a flick with a napkin and began to gather up the dirty cups and saucers.

'The usual, Mr. Hennessy?'

'The usual, with plenty of tea, and strong for the love of Mike. What do you want with your tea, Lou?'

'Just bread and butter, thanks.'

Tom dismissed the waitress with a wave of his hand.

'What age are you?'

'Twenty-two.'

'What have you been doing?'

I told him.

'Hum! I see! Can you type, do shorthand, keep an office tidy?'

'No, but I can learn.'

'Don't. What you never know you never have to do. Can you cook?'

'No, I want a newspaper job, not a husband.'

'I've known cookery appreciated even in the unmarried. Do you know anything about women's clothes, babies' teeth, diseases of infants, how to make yesterday's lunch into to-morrow's dinner, how to get rid of your mother-in-law with good feeling on both sides? In other words, have you any idea of how to run a woman's page?'

'None.' I was getting annoyed at his banter. Was I being baited to provide this fool with some amusement? Or was he going to help me?

'Well, I suppose you can read. The secret of successful journalism is not knowing things but knowing where to go for them. Now look here. I might manage to get Moriarty to work you in on the Woman's Page. At present it's done or supposed to be done by a dame called Mary Jeffreys. She's a big woman with the temper of the devil himself, but a decent soul; always at loggerheads with Moriarty. I'll suggest that you be put in under her to train. Now you must think of a bright idea. He's worked on American papers and he's strong on bright ideas. I'll tell Mary that she's being disgracefully overworked and needs an assistant. So long as you don't want to cover the race meetings she'll leave you alone.'

He took a copy of the paper from his pocket, opened it at the Woman's Page and handed it to me.

'Any bright ideas?'

I began to laugh. 'My head feels like a turnip.'

'Now for God's sake don't dry up in front of the boss. He's no respect for silent reserve or quiet strength. Here,' he looked the page through with a critical eye. 'What about some French cooking for the harassed housewife? You can read French, I suppose? And there's nothing on infant feeding in hot weather.'

'I suppose I can buy a book on that, too.'

'You're getting wise. You must produce several new lines for Moriarty. He'll forget about them afterwards. I've got it. Advice to lonely souls in the great city. There's no time like the present. Drink up your tea and come along.'

'Will Mr. Moriarty be in?'

'Of course he's in. He's always in. He lives in the office. You see he doesn't drink and when he has nothing to do he has to go home and talk to his wife. Naturally he prefers work.'

Tom Hennessy walked back with me to the newspaper offices and led me past the guileless young man at the desk who had the impertinence to smile at me and nod as if I were an old friend.

There was only one smell in the editor's room, tobacco. The atmosphere of the small room was so laden that it hurt the eyes. The windows were tightly closed and I suspected so was the chimney. The floor, desk, chairs were laden with a litter of papers and cuttings. Mr. Moriarty sat at the other side of the desk contemplating the disorder.

'Shut the door,' he shouted as we came in. 'There's a draught.'

Tom Hennessy shut it. I was always incapable of movement if anyone shouted at me.

'What do you want, young lady?' he asked grimly.

Tom Hennessy introduced me, spoke eloquently of my accomplishments and intelligence, and left me to continue myself. I stammered out a few words and then dried up.

'No, little girl,' said the editor, not unkindly. 'I'm afraid this is not your job.'

Tom jerked me in the ribs. I was not to give in.

Closing my eyes I took a long breath and thinking I might as well be hanged for a sheep as a lamb, I began:

'I am not the only one, Mr. Moriarty, who has been struck by the dullness of the Woman's Page.'

'So you think it dull. Well, run along and tell that to Mary Jeffreys and see what she has to say about it. Have you any suggestions to make, might I ask?'

I launched into a list of ideas, French cookery, lonely souls, lovers' column, hints to gardeners and ended up by saying that I had seen an exhibition of educational toys for children in London and wanted to know why the papers knew nothing about it.

The toys worked the oracle. Mr. Moriarty was a family man. I had not been to London. I had not seen the exhibition. I had read about it in a woman's paper while in the dentist's waiting-room. I was asked for a detailed description of the toys. Mr. Moriarty was delighted.

'We'll try you out. Take her along, Hennessy, and introduce her to Mary Jeffreys. She can begin to-morrow. I daren't face the woman. She's threatening to sue me for criminal slander. She's been in here suggesting that she knew more about me than was good for me, and God knows I lead a blameless enough life. If she as much as shows her nose in here I'll have her arrested for intimidation. Come and see me, young woman, when you've any smart ideas. I'm always pleased to hear them.'

'Were you at that exhibition?' Tom Hennessy asked as we went down the stairs.

'No.'

'I thought not. It sounded too convincing. I'm afraid you'll have to wait until to-morrow morning to meet Mary. She's at the Naas races.'

'I hope they are not going to sack her,' I said modestly.

'Sack Mary? Never. Moriarty tried it once. He didn't actually face her. He wrote her a letter the day he went on his summer holidays. She just tore it up and dropped it in the waste-paper basket and went on as usual. She was there when he came back. He hasn't tried it since.'

I GOT on well with Mary Jeffreys, a formidable but good-hearted woman with a passion for horse-racing. She was quick and capable at her work and I learned much from her. She bullied and petted me by turns but she taught me my job. Most of her free time was taken up picking winners, or losers, and talking to the Sports Editor about probable runners, weights, lengths, handicaps and jockeys. She had her favourites among the jockeys and like all punters she was extremely superstitious.

'I always like to back Joe Canty at the Park,' she would say. 'Morny Wing is at his best at Punchestown. I don't think I'll have much on to-day. I caught my toe in the mat as I came out of the house this morning.'

'Ever tried picking them out with a pin, Mary?' Tom Hennessy asked her.

'I put my faith in science. It's the man who studies form who comes out on top. Breeding counts in horse — and man.'

'It's the bookie who comes out on top, my love. If only punters put half as much energy, calculation and brains into any other business they'd be rich men.'

'Get along with you, Tom. You've no sporting instincts.'

After a bad day she would storm through the

office abusing everyone from the office boys to the editor and making the most outrageous threats. When her rage was exhausted, she would sink down on a chair, which creaked under her weight, sigh, and remark to me:

'Girleen, a word from the wise. The only way to follow a horse with profit is to follow it with a brush and shovel.'

The next day she was reading the lists of probable runners with the same eager excitement.

I felt happy in the offices of the *Evening Recorder*, not because the work was very interesting. The atmosphere of a newspaper office is friendly and impersonal and there men and women are liked not so much for their worth as for their kindliness towards their fellow-men.

Tom Hennessy regarded me as his protégée and responsibility. I was praised and blamed, warned and comforted by turns. We had long arguments and Tom took care to impress on me that in spite of my expensive education, I was a poor ignorant creature politically. He lectured me, read to me, took me to meetings until they were banned, and gave me dozens of books to read. In case I should have returned them unread with a polite 'Thank you', I had to stand an examination on each of them and all the questions raised were carefully argued to and fro.

'In a few years,' he would say, 'you'll know something about the subject. You're not doing too badly.'

Sometimes, when he had a free afternoon, he would 'show me the town'. This excursion always began by going to the lounge of the Shelborne or Hibernian for a drink. There he would point out to me the various people of importance who came in and out. From jockeys to government officials he knew them all.

'A good newspaper woman,' he said one day, 'should be able to recognize everyone. She should be able to remember faces, voices, names, clothes.'

After that we would either wander through the streets or go to the theatre. He was the pleasantest companion in the world.

On one of these excursions we strayed down the quays as far as the North Wall, Tom's favourite walk. He loved talking to the dockers and chatting with the foreign sailors who lounged about this quarter. We stood for a while watching a boat being loaded, then walked on.

'Did you notice those fellows looking at you?' Tom asked.

'Yes. Why?'

'I suppose you think it was your pretty face?'

'Wasn't it?'

'Naw!' Tom made a gesture of disgust with his hands. 'It was those clothes of yours. They didn't notice what you looked like except, maybe, that you were too thin. They weren't admiring you.'

'Why did they look at me, then?'

'Because they hated you.'

'They didn't. They don't know me.' I was piqued and annoyed. 'Why should anyone hate me?'

'They hate you because they can never possess you. They look at your fine clothes, your gentle appearance and compare you with their own women.'

I was silent. What Tom had said was probably true and it hurt me. This simple observation on his part brought home to me more than all his arguments the false foundations of society. It showed me how wrong values warped the lives of men and women and debased their relationship to one another.

As we walked to the end of the quays and stood for a few minutes looking out over the cold grey water of the bay, Tom continued talking:

'The economists and the historians tell us it was the lust of gold that drove men out over dangerous seas and into unknown places. It wasn't, Lou, not altogether. These scientific gentlemen always seem to forget the human factor. It was the lust of strange women, women with gold hair or gold skin. Women love gold as much as men, but if it had been left to them, America would never have been discovered.'

'You're talking nonsense, Tom. What about the Yukon gold rush? You don't mean to tell me it was the lure of the Esquimaux women that drew them on into that wilderness.'

'They didn't go there to stay there. They went to get gold, but what did they mean to do with it? Buy women they could not get otherwise.'

'As usual you're spoiling a good idea by overstatement. You always let your imagination run away with you. There are men who love money for itself, men who love money for the power it brings with it, men who do not care for women at all.'

'There are. But they're crazy, abnormal, every one of them. The normal man is ruled from cradle to grave by women. He struggles all his life to get away but he never can.'

'Then there are a great number of abnormal men.'

'There are, Lou, worse luck.'

At the Pillar we climbed on top of a tram to go home. Another couple came and sat down in front of us. The man was from the country, probably a farmer. He was a heavily built, rather handsome fellow who would fall into flesh when he was a little older. The woman was middle aged and had the grey colour of those who seldom go abroad in daylight, probably a cousin who had come to town to become a dressmaker. She must have been a relative because he was discussing with her the problem of 'settling down'.

'Now,' he remarked. 'I could maybe get a girl with three hundred and she mightn't have such a good character as a girl with only two hundred. Now, I'd take the girl with the two hundred. That's the sort of man I am.'

'You're right,' answered the woman.

'Your adventurous man,' I whispered.

'Isn't he grand,' sighed Tom. 'The backbone of the country! The romantic Irishman!'

'Did he ever exist?' I asked.

'He didn't.'

I lived at that time in a small flat right at the top of a large house in a street just off Stephen's Green. Except for the top story it was given over to offices. The ground floor was taken up by a turf accountant.

'You've never been to my flat, Tom. There's some food in the larder. Come up and I'll give you some supper.'

Tom stood for a moment looking at the windows.

'I'm coming up,' he answered. 'I want to have a look at it.'

These were the years when Mr. Lloyd George, having won the Great War and the Hang-the-Kaiser Election, was turning his attention to Ireland. If he could only settle the Irish question, he would have done what no man had been able to do for seven hundred years. There was nothing new in the methods he adopted. They were those of Mountjoy, and had been tried many times before, always with the same result. He flooded the country with the Black and Tans, a war-crazed and brutal soldiery.

For some time I had suspected Tom Hennessy of being one of the men who took part in the guerrilla war waged against them. I never asked him, nor did he tell me. The better I knew him, the more convinced I became. His work did not tie him to the office during regular hours. He was free to go and come when he liked and his press card was a passport to unlikely places.

When he entered my flat, he looked carefully around. He examined the position of the doors, the stairs, the bedroom, sitting-room, bathroom and kitchen.

'Does that skylight open?' he asked, pointing to the window over the bath.

'I don't know. I never tried.'

He pushed it open. A shower of dirt and plaster fell into the bath.

'Look what you've done,' I exclaimed.

'Sorry, Lou. I'm going out on the roof if you don't mind.'

'Please yourself, but hadn't you better take off your coat. Then you'll only have to pay for having the trousers cleaned.'

I was putting the supper on the table when he came back.

'I'll send a good carpenter round to-morrow to fix that skylight. I want it to open and shut easily. I also want some bolts on it. Have you got a spare set of keys?'

'Yes. Why?'

'They might come in useful. Hand them over. I'll promise they'll never fall into irresponsible hands. If you hear noises in your sitting-room at night, don't get up and investigate. Say to yourself, it's only rats. Still and all, you might keep your bedroom door locked. If you are raided by Black and Tans, go into the bathroom before you open the door and shoot the bolt in the skylight. I think the front door might be strengthened, too. I don't want them breaking in.'

'And I don't want Black and Tans to come raiding my place. I'm all alone here.'

'Get a telephone installed. The moment they enter your place, ring up police headquarters and complain. They won't touch you, then. One thing more. Keep yourself clear of all political organizations. Don't get known.'

I looked at Tom and I was frightened.

'You're playing this game with a rope round your neck.'

'We must all wear a necktie of one kind or another. It is an evil thing to lie on another man's bones.'

From then, I often heard stealthy movements in my sitting-room at night. Sometimes I felt inclined to get up and talk to my unknown visitor, but I remembered Tom's warning, given, I was sure, because he felt it safer that I should not know whom I was harbouring. When I got up in the morning he was always gone. One morning I opened the bedroom door earlier than usual. A stranger was sleeping in one of the chairs, his head on the crook of his arm which rested on the table. He must have been very uncomfortable, I thought. I should have ordered a divan for the unknown guest. The stranger turned and his arm slipped from under his head. He sat up, rubbing his face with his hands. It was Egan O'Doherty.

I NO longer locked my bedroom door. When Egan came, as he did at least twice a week, I was waiting for him. Sometimes he was so exhausted that he fell asleep while I was getting him something to eat. At other times he was so excited that he would talk half the night. When I bought a divan for him, he laughed.

'Hell, I can sleep anywhere. I've slept in muddy trenches, on the side of the road, in leaky barns. An old campaigner doesn't need a bed.'

From the day when I walked out of my bedroom and found him asleep, I lived in fear. Every rumour of a fight, of a round-up, of an ambush filled me with dread. It was bad enough to know that he might be shot, but the more terrible thought that he might be stopped and caught with a revolver dwelt eternally in my mind. 'To be hanged by the neck until you are dead.'

As I waited for him at night, I could see, as clearly as if I were there, the horrible grey morning in Mountjoy Prison, the hangman's hands on his throat. One nightmare vision chased another through my mind. When he did not come I wandered restlessly through the flat, my ears strained to catch, in the silence of the quiet city, the bursting crash of bombs and the rattle of shots. The whine of the passing lorries sent all the blood in my body to my heart and I shivered with terror. I stood at the window listening until the sound of the engine had faded into the dark distance. When I heard the key turn in the lock, my knees weakened under me and I felt faint with joy and relief. I thought of those other wives and sweethearts and wondered how women can go on enduring this agony from one day to another.

A love that is born in fear is a terrible and possessive love.

One night a thunderstorm broke over the city. I got up and closed the window for the rain was beating in. As I was getting back to bed, the bedroom door opened and Egan stood in the doorway. He did not speak, but in the uncertain light I was aware of the hysterical glitter in his eyes. I crawled in under the sheet, at the same time stretching out one hand towards him. He threw himself down on the bed beside me, dragging the clothes over him, burying his head on my shoulder and holding me tightly in his arms. For a long time, neither of us spoke. At last, when the roll of the thunder was faint in the distance, he lifted his head and said:

'You must forgive me, Lou. I can't endure thunder. It's too like the guns in France. They went on and on until you were deaf and dumb and blind.'

'Why do you still go on fighting?'

'I'm an old soldier, now. When I see a fight I must get into it. I don't feel safe otherwise.'

I said nothing to Tom Hennessy about all this. I

154

did not even tell him that I knew the man who had taken refuge in my room. He guessed it. Perhaps some change in my manner gave me away for I was often distraught and worried and my temper was easily roused. Even Mary Jeffreys noticed it and suggested a holiday.

'Where could I go?' I asked sharply. 'It's the same everywhere.'

'You could go to England or France.'

'If I met an Englishman now, I'd strangle him, and France is too far off. Anything might happen while I was away.'

'It would happen anyway, dear,' her voice was kind and gentle. 'Your being here or there won't prevent it.'

'I won't go,' I answered obstinately.

Tom Hennessy was standing near, waiting for me. As we walked along the street he said suddenly:

'You know Egan O'Doherty?'

'I grew up in the same village.'

'Strange you should have breathed the same air and grown up in innocence.'

'Stop ragging, Tom. What have you against him?'

'As man to man, nothing.'

'Are you trying to warn me?'

'If there's one thing a man hates doing, it is warning a woman against another man, particularly when that man is a friend of his. It makes him feel such a prig. As I said, I've got nothing against him. I like his cold, clear, ruthless intelligence. I admire his capacity for deceiving others and yet not for a moment deceiving himself. He has a quality which draws my heart towards him and when I look at him, I see something in those beautiful blue eyes I only see in the eyes of a woman. But to those who do not understand him, to women especially, he is as unscrupulous and treacherous as a rattlesnake. More, a rattlesnake rattles.'

'Why did you send him to me?'

'I did not know that he knew you. He never told me. I put him under oath to leave you alone. You see, he has few friends here and I wanted him to be safe. If he were taken, little mercy would be shown him. He's an old soldier. Will I get you back your keys?'

'No. It would be no use now. Tom, do you remember one evening when we were coming home together on the top of the tram, the evening you came to my flat? There was a fellow from the country talking about the sort of woman he would marry.'

'I remember.'

'We made the astounding discovery that my good character was worth one hundred pounds. Well, I've more than that in the bank.'

'Well, be sure that your horse is trying when you lay your money.' He grinned maliciously and slapped me on the shoulder.

Tom Hennessy had underrated two things, my obstinacy and Egan's honesty. Night after night he told me of adventures he had had, women he had known. He never once tried to excuse himself, to justify his conduct. He never even offered an explanation. I sat beside him, hugging my knees for comfort, my soul tortured by every word he said. But my feet were caught fast in the quicksand. Knowledge never saved any woman.

I think that Tom must have said something to him, for one evening he came to my flat early. He was restless and silent. There was a cold light in his eyes I had not so far seen.

'What ails you?' I asked.

'Huh!' He looked at me as if he had not heard.

'What's the matter?'

'Matter?' He tightened his lips over his teeth and looked down at his boots. 'I've come to say good-bye.'

'Good-bye? Why?'

'I'm leaving. Good-bye. Thanks for everything.'

I said nothing. For the life of me I could not utter a word. He stood at the end of the table as if half asleep. I made no movement to approach him. Slowly he put his hand in his breast pocket and took out his wallet. From it he took a photograph I had given him, a photograph of myself as a little girl, standing in my aunt's rose-garden, smiling happily. He threw it down on the table and strode out of the flat.

Overcome by despair, I sank down on the floor. I had never known such pain. An ecstasy of grief swept over me, submerging me like a heavy sea. It robbed me of all feeling of reality, carried me away in a wild emotion, almost of pleasure. This is the end, I thought, the end of life, the end of living. I shall go away, go on and on and on, for ever.

A hand was laid on my shoulder.

'Lou, little Lou.'

I looked up. He was smiling. Slowly he sat down on the floor beside me.

'You haven't gone,' I stammered.

'And never will, so long as I live, sweet. When I got to the foot of the stairs, I knew that life without you was a bare and desolate waste. Little Lou, I am all yours.'

I began to weep and wring my hands. Wild, hysterical sobs shook me from head to foot. I could not stop them.

'Don't cry! Please, darling, don't cry! I can't bear you to cry. Smile, little love, my own love, my only love.'

I HANDED in my copy and left the office. It was a warm spring day and the soft wind from the hills was blowing little white clouds across the sky, so I decided to walk to the small restaurant where I usually ate, instead of taking the tram. I wandered up Grafton Street, looking at the shop windows, humming a tune. Because the morning had been chilly I had brought a little black fur muff with me and I now carried it under my arm, letting the sun warm my bare hands. When I came near Noblett's corner, I remembered that I wanted some paper and started to cross the street. Half-way across I heard the first explosion, quickly followed by another. I knew what it was, an ambush opposite the College of Surgeons, a favourite point of attack. Before I had time to think I was across the street and inside a café.

There was a little crowd there and as the rattle of bullets began, more joined. We pressed together, waiting for the attack to be over. Men with sullen faces stood around, their hands rammed deep into their pockets. Women crossed themselves and prayed. There was a horrible silence, interrupted only by the sound of rifle and revolver fire and a last explosion. Three bombs, I counted. Then it was all over.

At first no one moved. One or two spoke in low

tones as if muttering. Then the waitresses began to pass to and fro, shouting their orders into the lift. I was leaning against the wall, watching the door. It swung open and a couple of men entered. I recognized Egan O'Doherty. He pushed his way through the crowd of women who were now talking hysterically and leaned against the wall beside me. I turned round with a smile, but there was no sign of recognition on his face. I was holding my muff in the hand next him and suddenly I became aware that a warm piece of metal was being slipped into it. It was his revolver which he pushed into my hand. I made no sign. He moved away.

I decided to stay where I was for lunch. It would be dangerous to walk through the streets with a loaded revolver, and I would have to return it somehow. As I moved towards one of the tables, a hand touched my shoulder. I turned round. A tall gaily dressed woman stood smiling at me. At first I did not recognize her, though she looked familiar. Then she laughed and I knew who she was. She was my cousin Justin's wife, Nell.

'Well,' she said, 'If it isn't little sobersides. How's life, dearie?'

Her voice was husky and broken but her smile was as gay as ever.

'Nell!' I exclaimed. 'This is the last place on earth I would have thought of meeting you. What on earth are you doing here?'

But before she could answer, the doors of the

restaurant burst open and a company of Auxiliary Police rushed in, revolvers in their hands. They came in red with anger, hungry for a victim. I guessed at once by their fierce swagger that one or more of their party had been killed. Inside my muff, my fingers clutched Egan O'Doherty's revolver. Were they going to search us, the women as well as the men? I wondered if I could slip away and drop the revolver through a window. But one glance and I knew that it was impossible.

'Hands up! Line up along the wall there!' the leader shouted. 'Pronto! Tout de sweet! Look slippy about it! Not a word out of one of you or I'll fill you full of lead. Pass along now, one by one. We're going to search every blasted man jack of you.'

I held up my hands, terrified that the muff would slip down over my arm and leave the revolver exposed to view. I didn't even dare look at it to see if the top were sticking out. At the same time I was glad I had it. It would mean a prison sentence if it were found on me but it would have been a hanging matter for Egan.

The officer walked up and down the line and when he came to where we were standing he halted. Nell was smiling at him. He tipped his cap with the point of his revolver.

'Say, Tom,' she said. 'You don't need to search us. This lady is my cousin.'

He nodded grimly and motioned us out of the ranks. Nell seized me by the elbow and dragged me to a table at the back of the room. Only when we sat down did I remember to lower my arms. I closed my eyes. My eyelids were heavy with moisture.

'What you need, dearie,' said Nell in a kindly voice, 'is a good stiff drink. What were you in such a funk about? They're not such bad fellows, you know. It's not the like of you they're after. Can I get you anything?'

'Nothing,' I replied, and then added, 'A cup of coffee.'

I watched the search. I could not take my eyes from those dark uniformed figures as they danced up and down the line of people, threatening them with their revolvers. Men and women were rudely pushed about, cursed at, searched. Practised hands felt them all over, handbags were opened and the contents strewn over the floor, pockets emptied, but nothing was found. Egan's companion must have managed to get rid of his revolver too. The Auxiliary Police left as suddenly as they had come, and with a flick of their aprons the waitresses returned to their tables as if nothing had happened.

Egan O'Doherty came over and sat at the table next to us. I looked at him but he did not even glance in my direction. He sat looking down on the table, drumming on it with his finger-nails. One of the waitresses approached the table and he looked up.

'Huh!' he said, looking at her stupidly.

'That was a nice how-do-ye-do,' she remarked.

'Very pretty,' he replied absent-mindedly and then added. 'You might bring me a cup of coffee, Katie, black and leave the bill.'

'Waitress,' Nell called.

The girl approached.

'Two cups of coffee. What would you like to eat, dearie?'

My gorge rose at the thought of food.

'Nothing. I can't eat.'

'Come along.' She leaned over me and patted me on the shoulder. I was overpowered by the smell of stale perfume and whisky. 'Pull yourself together and have a bite of something. 'Twill do you good.' She glanced at the menu. 'Liver and bacon for two.'

I knew that the longer I stayed here, the better. If I went out now I might be held up in the street and searched. Reluctantly I took my hand out of the muff and laid it on the table. It was shaking. I forced myself to pay some attention to Nell.

Though she must have been still in the twenties, she had aged considerably. Her face, which was heavily made up, had coarsened and lined and her figure was getting heavy. Only her smile was as young and naive as ever, and she still had beautiful teeth. I could see by the high pitched tone of her voice and the looseness of her movements that she had been drinking that morning already. She seemed really pleased to have met me but I doubted if she would have spoken to me at all if she had not been a little drunk.

'It's good to see you again,' she was saying with great enthusiasm. 'How are you getting along?'

'Fine!' I answered. 'I'm working on a paper now.'

'Do you like it? Do they pay you decently?'

'Oh, it's quite interesting and I make enough to live and a bit over.'

'Better than standing on your feet all day, anyway. That's how I began, in a café.'

'Was it awful?' I asked for want of something better to say.

'I didn't stick it long. Said I to myself, better bed sores than varicose veins. Any news of Justin?'

'No. Is he here?'

'How should I know? Haven't seen him for years.'

'What wind blew you over to Ireland? You must find it dull here, what with a war on and curfew and all.'

'Well, I was sort of tied up with a fellow and he was under marching orders, so I came over with him. It's not so bad here. The fellows are all right when they take time off from running about knocking off Sinn Feiners. They've good pay and they don't mind spending it. And the lads of the village aren't so bad either.'

'Don't talk so loudly, Nell.' I spoke in a low voice, slowly and insistently.

She lowered her voice.

'Your nerves are all shot to pieces, dearie. There's no one about but that bloke at the next table and he looks as if he could hardly tell you his name.' She glanced at Egan O'Doherty. 'Though mind you, he's not so bad looking. I've got a nice little flat here. Come round and be cheered up. You must meet Jim. I'll give a party and ask along some of the boys.'

'Jim?'

'He's the bloke I came over with. I'm living with him now. A bit tough now and then when he has a load on, but decent as men go. I know how to manage him. He's not like Justin. He's the sort can give and take.'

Her voice was rising again.

'What's happened to Justin?'

'Don't ask me, dearie. He never needed me to look after him. He could do that himself. But don't you ever hear from him?'

'The last letter I got was from Malta.'

'He's got around a bit since then. Shedding his illusions, he used to say. Talked as if they were his underpants.'

'So you haven't seen him for some time?'

'And let me tell you, dearie, I don't want to. Though I always do say it for Justin, he could be good fun when he was wound up. But he had such a habit of coming unstuck in your hands. He was — he was — ' she searched about for a word. 'He was kind of awkward.'

'That's true enough.'

'Oh, let's leave him. No good harking back, is

there? Tell me, how are you? Ever think of getting married?'

'Sometimes, Nell. But never long enough to have the banns put up.'

'That's a pity. If you did yourself up a bit and bought yourself some glad rags, you'd knock them flat. Still, you're getting about a bit, I suppose. Plenty of nice fellows about. But do come round to my place and meet a few of them. It's 74 Marshall Street, second floor. The boys feel a bit lonely sometimes and would like to meet a nice girl.'

I glanced at the table next to us. Egan had finished his coffee and had lit a cigarette. He was quietly tearing an empty cigarette packet to pieces. I knew he was listening.

'No, thanks, Nell. I don't think I will. But come round to the office and see me. We could go out somewhere. You see — I don't much like Black and Tans.'

'Oh, all right,' she answered, not taking the hint. 'But Jim's not one of them, dearie. He's not an ordinary fellow, you see. He's clever and a gentleman. He's really quite important.'

I kicked her under the table but it was too late. I prayed that Egan had not heard. Nell apparently imagined that I was not sufficiently impressed, and went on:

'He's a real gentleman, an officer, doing secret Government work over here. Do come round. You'll like him. His name's Captain James Musgrave. Be

166

sure to ask for Mrs. Musgrave. That's my name now.'

I looked round at Egan O'Doherty. He was still tearing the cigarette box up into very small pieces. He was looking absent-mindedly across the restaurant.

'Don't talk nonsense, Nell,' I said abruptly. 'Look here. I'm working on the *Evening Recorder*. Come along some day at five o'clock and we'll go out together. I must get back now.'

'Right you are, dearie. We'll hit the high spots. We'll make this little old town look up and shake itself.'

We separated at the door of the restaurant. I crossed into Stephen's Green. As I stood on the bridge watching the ducks playing in the water, Egan O'Doherty came and leaned over the bridge beside me.

'Thanks for looking after the gat, Lou. You can hand it over now.'

I pushed the muff towards him.

'Tell me,' he asked, 'who was the dame who came to your rescue?'

'Oh, just someone I met years ago. I don't remember her name.'

'Don't bother to tell lies, Lou. She's your cousin's wife.'

'She used to be.'

'What's she doing now?'

'How should I know?'

'I see.'

'Egan!' I turned round and took one of his hands. 'Forget it, will you? She's just a silly fool. She doesn't understand anything of what's going on — and she's Justin's wife.'

'I see. You don't want Justin's name dragged into this.' He slipped my hand under his arm and walked along beside me. 'But Lou, if you yourself, even you, my sweet, my pretty Lou, were to — how shall I say it? — were to take government money for information received, I'd — shoot you down like a dog. Don't you realize what such women are here for? They're sent out to see what they can pick up, and believe me, they earn their money.'

'Egan,' I pleaded. 'She would harm no one. She has a kind heart. All she ever wants is a good time. Forget it. You know, I might have been caught with that gun.'

'You might, that's true. I'm not forgetting that. I was in a cold sweat when I saw they were lining up the women too. But for you, I'd have made a pretty picture at the end of a rope. Still, I had no choice, they wouldn't have hanged you.'

Suddenly I could see him dangling at the end of a rope. My heart skipped a beat.

'Then, for my sake, forget it.'

He turned round and looked at me. His blue eyes smiled at me — the bluest eyes I have ever seen.

'For your sake, sweet,' he said softly, 'I'd forget almost anything.'

Then he bent down and kissed me.

Two days later I opened an evening paper. The first thing I saw was a heading:

BRITISH OFFICER AND HIS WIFE MURDERED IN BED

    This morning two armed men entered the flat of Captain James Musgrave ...

I did not need to read the rest. I knew. I rushed back into the building, looking for Tom Hennessy. I found him joking with Bill Cairns, the news editor.

'Tom,' I said. 'Come here a moment.'

He followed me into the corridor.

'What's the matter, Lou?'

'Where's Egan O'Doherty?'

'Now, for God's sake, child, calm yourself. He's had to leave town for a couple of days. Don't get yourself worked up. You're not the only girl who'll be crying her eyes out over that son of a bitch.'

'Stop fooling, Tom. Tell me, where is he?'

Tom Hennessy hesitated and then answered in a low voice.

'Keep it under your hat, Lou. The powers that be, you know, the higher command or whatever you call it, thought he needed a holiday, so he's been sent on an ocean voyage. At this moment he's probably in a stokehold, working his passage to America. Got out this morning. Told me to give you his love.'

'Judas!' I cried. 'Judas!'

'And Iscariot!' added Tom. 'But don't say you weren't warned.'

It wasn't until after the Treaty was signed and the Civil War threatened us that Egan O'Doherty returned. If Tom Hennessy heard from him or about him, he said nothing to me. I suppose he thought that the sooner Egan faded from my thoughts the better. Or perhaps he did not hear anything. But one day when I turned up at the office, Tom, who had been up the night before at a Dail debate, was sitting waiting for me. He was leaning forward in the chair, his elbows on his knees, twirling his hat in his hands. He looked up without raising his body. His long red face was even more gloomy than usual.

'He's back,' he remarked.

'Who?'

'The ten plagues of Egypt, the scourge of the seven seas, the terror that flieth by night.'

'I suppose you must be referring to Egan O'Doherty. It can't be Tim Healy. He hasn't been out of town. They're the only two who appear to be able to rouse you to such a pitch of eloquence. Where did you see him?'

'In Mooneys-en-ville.'

'What's he doing?'

'Can't say yet. He was drinking whisky when I saw him. He refused to be drawn on the subject of his future movements. He talked feelingly about a great new force that was being born and would sweep down from the hills and engulf and drown all the little men, leaving, I suppose, Egan O'Doherty standing on a mountain.'

'There's probably some sense in what he is saying, though it sounds obscure and involved at times. He's very like the celebrated Delphic oracle. He'll go Republican.'

'Now, how do you know that?'

'Because Tom, my dear, he always takes the long view. It won't be from fiery conviction, as might happen in your case, but because of some inverted reasoning of his own, propelled perhaps by this cosmic force he has just discovered. He will argue that by supporting the Republicans he is following Connolly's teaching, though Connolly being dead now, anyone can put words into his mouth. Or again he may argue that the victory of Republicanism is the death of Imperialism and consequently of Capitalism. But it won't be logical to anyone else.'

'How well you know him.' Tom smiled.

'Tom,' I asked, 'did you ever realize a man was cheating you and let him do it?'

'No, why should I do that?'

'Because, I suppose, you were getting something out of it he didn't suspect you were getting.'

'Well, in that case it's a double cheat and cancels itself out. It's foolish to be too clever. That's what's the matter with O'Doherty. He's so clever that his thoughts go in spirals. He can't see straight. He can reason himself into anything — and out again. He's a snake eating its own tail.'

'This time he'll probably reason himself into a thoroughly good mess. When this storm breaks, it will swamp the country.'

'The country's behind us, Lou.'

'Don't kid yourself. It's not. The country wants peace. And as far as I can judge, and what is more significant, the I.R.B. wants peace.'

'This isn't what we fought for.'

'No, Tom, and I don't expect you'll ever get what you fought for. Take what you can get and don't be grateful.'

'Lou, you wouldn't go back on us?'

'No. I just hate what I see coming. It will put back what we both want for generations. We hoped that out of this struggle the working class would seize power. It was a smoke dream. Free State or Republic, what does it matter? The little tradesman will have his day, and the big industrialist will have his, and the worker will go to the wall. Listen, Tom, before all this bitterness and quibbling swamps our reason and makes it impossible for us to talk and act like civilized human beings, let us ask ourselves what we really want? What is your ultimate aim?'

'You know, Lou. A workers' republic.'

'Sounds fine. But will a republic bring us any nearer that? Please don't get angry with me, Tom. You have all my loyalty. The things you want are the things I want, but we're going to see ourselves fighting for something very different. But let's at least look at it with our eyes open. The Irish Capitalist when he comes is no more our friend than the English Capitalist, but the English worker could be our brother. In reality he is fighting for the same ideal.'

'But only by settling this national question, by freeing Ireland, can we hope to get on with our struggle.'

'You may think so, but I don't. However, go about it your own way but don't blame me for doubting it to be the best way.'

'But de Valera says . . . '

'Tom. De Valera is a politician. He loves words. You may call him an honest man. He may be, according to his lights. But his ways are not our ways and his aims are not ours, no more than Michael Collins's are. He plans to found a bourgeois republic in which we shall wear Irish tweeds and eat Irish porridge and grow Irish wheat at great expense and labour at the expense of the Irish worker. He may win, he may get it, but I don't think so. His attitude to Labour will be no better than that of Griffith and Collins. Worse maybe. Mussolini is nearer his ideal than Lenin. And, don't forget it, he is a devout and believing Catholic.'

'What has that to do with it?'

'You ask me that, Tom Hennessy. Have you forgotten all you have said? You know what the attitude of the Church is to Labour. De Valera himself would be the last to deny it.'

'Is it any better in the Protestant Church?'

'Not a bit, so don't run away with the idea that it's my Protestant blood speaking. It is you yourself speaking, Tom. The one thing I want you to remember is this. I am neither Free State nor Republican. I am what you have made me, a Socialist, and I've always thought that you were one. It will be difficult for us to get through the next couple of years without many misunderstandings, but before the storm breaks I want you to know what I really think and I want to know if you think the same. Are you first and foremost a Socialist or are you a Republican?'

He was silent for a moment.

'It's strange, Lou. It was I who taught you, read to you, preached at you, gave you Socialist pamphlets to read, educated you, and now you are the one to turn on me. Serves me right in a way. If I'd made love to you instead of worrying about your political education, you'd maybe not be looking at me now with that cold and critical eye. But honesty for honesty. I'm afraid I am first of all a Republican. The old hatred of England has eaten into my bones. It is stronger than anything else.'

'Well, there we are and we know. Let it rest. Now, no matter what happens, Tom, nothing can spoil our friendship. Tell me, was Egan as close about his past as he was about his future? He didn't tell you by any chance what he'd been doing this past year?'

'Not a word, and believe me it's maybe just as well. We're hardened warriors in Mooney's, but our souls are not altogether seared. There are some things better not spoken.' He grinned again.

'Did he say he was coming round?'

'If you mean, Lou, did he ask how you were, he didn't. He didn't as much as mention your name. Maybe he's forgotten it. In that case you're lucky.'

But Tom Hennessy was wrong. That evening as I left the building to go home, Egan was standing outside waiting for me. My heart nearly choked me when I saw him.

'Come along and have a bite, Lou,' he said and his blue eyes smiled. 'I want to hear what you have to say about the present situation. Where the hell can we eat in this one-horse town at this time of night?'

He took my arm and led me towards O'Connell Street. It was a couple of minutes before I could speak.

'You're always hungry,' I said at last.

'I've been hungry, maybe that's the reason.'

Now that I saw him again, I forgot that I was angry with him, I forgot that he was a liar and a cheat, I forgot that I had sworn never to forgive him for Nell's death, I forgot that I was never going to speak to him again. All resentment faded from my mind. I was happy that he had come to see me, happy to see him smile.

When the Civil War broke out both Tom Hennessy and Egan O'Doherty disappeared. I was, of course, like many others, in complete ignorance of the cross currents and undercurrents of Irish politics at that time. I knew that we did not know or hear everything and that every body, secret and public, was split on the issue of the Treaty. Families were divided, brother against brother, father against son. But the mass of the people was tired and apathetic. The common man had had his bellyfull of fighting and wanted peace.

Neither came to say good-bye. I had a note from Tom, telling me that they were going, and a letter from Egan which told me nothing. He wrote:

'Nothing is certain, sweet one, but that I will come back.'

Very little news trickled through. Occasionally a country fellow would arrive at my door late at night, saying that Tom Hennessy had sent him. When he had rested and eaten, he would give me his message and disappear again. But the message contained nothing but an assurance that he was still alive and well. From Egan I heard nothing. What news I got, I got from Mary Jeffreys. The racing fraternity is large and varied, drawn from every class and shade of opinion. She had heard that Egan was active in Clare. Tom was in Kerry at the head of a flying column and was having a hard time. The approach of winter would drive him down from the hills to the small towns and villages where his enemies lay waiting.

Then, one autumn evening I had definite news of Tom. I arrived home and found a tired-looking young woman sitting on the step outside the door of my flat. She rose when she saw me.

'Are you Miss Delahaie?' she asked.

'Yes, do you wish to see me? Come in.'

'My name is Delia Hennessy.'

'You've got a message for me from Tom? This way. Do sit down.'

She refused.

'What I have to say may be best said standing. I've brought you this.'

She held out a man's gold watch. It was Tom's. I took it and looked at it.

'He is dead,' I said.

'God rest his soul,' answered Delia Hennessy. 'They sent us his clothes and wallet and his watch. My mother and I thought you might like to have the watch.'

I pushed it back.

'I can't take it. You are not rich people. I cannot tell you how sorry I am . . .' I could not go on. My voice sounded so dead and inhuman.

'I know. But what does it matter that we are poor. Tom would have liked you to have something to remember him by. We're not likely to forget him. Keep it.'

I lifted the watch again. How often I had seen it in Tom's hands. They could not have sent me anything that I valued more. I went across the room to my desk. It was impossible to offer the girl the price of the watch yet I knew that they must be desperately poor now that Tom was gone. I took my grandmother's gold chain from her old jewel box and held it out to Delia Hennessy.

'Would it be too much to ask of you to take this from Tom's old friend?'

She shook her head but she did not take it off when I placed it round her neck.

'Tell me,' I asked, 'how was he killed and where?'

'We know nothing,' she answered. But whether she lied or not I could not say, her face was so still. It was no great matter. That Tom was dead was in itself terrible enough. She refused to stay any longer.

'I'd best be getting home to my mother,' she replied.

'Promise me one thing,' I asked. 'If you need help, will you let me know? Tom would have helped me.'

She looked at me. Her eyes were dry and hard with grief.

'I will,' she answered. But I knew that she never would. No one had the right to help them but their own.

I waited now for news of Egan. It came sooner than I dared expect. Early one morning, a letter, delivered by hand, was pushed through my letter

179

box. Evidently he did not trust the post. He asked me to meet him that afternoon at the terminus of the number fourteen tram.

When I got off the tram, I stood alone looking around me. Not until the tram had moved off again did he emerge from the shelter of a garden. He took my arm and we walked together to a little park near-by. I looked up at his face under the brim of the grey hat he was wearing. To my surprise he looked gay and happy.

'Come,' he said. 'Sit down here.'

'No, let us walk, it's cold.' There was a light frost and the ground crackled under our feet.

'Sit down,' he demanded, stopping opposite a wooden bench. 'There's something I want to ask you.'

I did as I was told. He sat beside me and took both my hands in his.

'Anne-Louise Delahaie, I want to ask you, will you marry me?'

I looked at his laughing eyes and asked myself, 'Is he serious?'

'Do you need to ask?' I replied.

'Answer me. Will you marry me?'

'I will.'

'I'm glad,' he answered simply. 'I was afraid you just mightn't. I was afraid you knew me too well, that you wouldn't trust me. Will you marry me right now?'

'What, to-day?'

'Or to-morrow.'

'When you will.'

'Lou, my sweet, come let's walk.' We walked up and down under the bare trees. The long winter twilight was closing in and the branches stood out against the clear sky like arms stretched out to heaven. We were all alone, alone in this garden, alone in the world.

'I've loved you a long time,' he said. 'Ever since one day I awoke and saw you standing looking at me. I said to myself — there's my wife. That is how true love comes, suddenly, like God's lightning. Do you know the old Irish poem?

When my hand was lifted at Mass to salute the Host,
I looked at you once and the half of my soul was lost.'

'Only half, Egan?'

'It's a lot, for an Irishman.'

He laughed. His eyes were dancing with joy. His arm which lay across my shoulders held me close. I shook my head.

'You have taken the east from me, and the west from me. You have taken the path before me and path behind me.'

'From this day on, love of my heart, we'll travel the same path. It may lead us into strange places, but always together. Will you be afraid?'

'No. Where does it lead now?'

'Away from here. France, Italy, America, where you will.'

'Why?'

'My life is not worth twenty-four hours' purchase in this town.'

'But I can't go at once. There are so many things to do. My flat, my job. I'll have to get some money from the bank. I've a thousand things to settle.'

'Leave them to settle themselves. Have your money transferred to London. We're getting out of here to-night. I hate to let you out of my sight, sweet one. Run along now and pack your bag and meet me on the boat.'

As he kissed me, I clapped my hands to his sides.

'Your gun, Egan. Give it me.'

'Ah no, Lou. My gat and I are never parted. If I die, I die fighting. Run along and get your things. I've enough money for us both.'

As we stood together at the rail, looking across Dublin Bay at the fading lights, he put his arm round me, his head close to mine, and said:

'We're setting out, you and I, on a brave adventure. Our ship is set, dear love, for a full due.'

PART III

EGAN AND JUSTIN

It was New Year's Eve and after dancing until nearly midnight I went on to another party where I was to meet Egan. I arrived very late to find that most of the merrymaking was over and a silence had fallen on the company. For, as often happens at such parties, everyone had paired off into some obscure corner of the large room. The air was full of whisperings and the lights were low. I looked around for Egan but he was nowhere to be seen. For a moment I wondered if by chance I had come to the wrong address, but no, I had taken it down carefully. Too shy and perhaps ashamed to look for him, I stood awkwardly in the middle of the room.

My hostess, whom I had never met, but who had sent me the invitation through Egan, disentangled herself from the embraces of a young man somewhere in the shadows and came forward. She bade me welcome in a sleepy voice and asked me what I would drink. Carelessly she poured me out a glass of whisky when I asked for sherry, and, smiling in that stupid way so many women do when they are both amorous and intoxicated, she moved back to her corner, leaving me there at the table by myself, wishing I had not come. I looked at the glass in my hand, at the rows of bottles on the table, at the dark curtained room and did not know what to do. I felt such a fool. I saw an empty chair at the far end of the room, and taking my glass, I moved over and sat down. I was very cold for there was a bitter east wind and I had got chilled in the taxi. I drew the chair up to the fire.

For some time I sat there alone, wondering why I had come and wishing with all my heart that I had the courage to get up and go away. But the east wind was howling and the warmth was comforting. I settled the cushions at my back and prepared to go to sleep.

Just as I was dozing off I felt a hand on my knee. Opening my eyes slowly I saw a man seated beside me on a cushion, a tall, broad-shouldered man with dark hair. He turned his head and smiled at me. Half-frightened, I leaned forward suddenly, my hand outstretched. It was my cousin Justin.

'Hallo, Miss Honeyball,' he said. 'A happy New Year!'

I stared at him, unable to utter a word. He had remained in my mind a tall, lanky boy and now I found him a strong, heavily built man. My mind could not bridge the years. Yet the dark eyes that smiled from under those straight black brows were the same and the lock of black hair that fell forward over his forehead.

'A happy New Year!' he said again.

I found my voice.

'Justin!'

'Sure, Loulie, your cousin Justin.'

'I can hardly believe it.'

He took my outstretched hand and held it in his.

'The very same, my dear. Tell me, what has brought you here?'

'A long series of events.'

'Why haven't you been to see me?'

'I didn't know that you were living in London, or I had forgotten. You belonged to another world, another life.'

'You're living here now?'

'Off and on.'

'What are you doing?'

'Free-lance, and I'm married.'

'Married? Oh, I suppose so. Who to?'

'To someone from home. Egan O'Doherty. You remember him?'

'Can't say that I do.'

'You must, Justin. He was the boy you nearly killed.'

'My God, how did you come to marry him?'

I shrugged my shoulders.

'Because I wanted to, I suppose.'

'Is he here? Where is he?'

'He was to meet me here but he hasn't turned up.'

My cousin glanced sharply at me.

Someone had put a record on the gramophone and one or two couples began to dance. There was movement now and the sound of voices.

'I say, Loulie, we can't talk here. It's a dull party, anyway. Come along to my house. I don't live far off.'

I hesitated.

'Afraid?' he asked. 'Why?'

The remark stung. I was afraid and I hated Justin for seeing it.

'Why should I be?' I hoped that my voice sounded reasonably indifferent. 'I merely thought that if Egan turned up, I had promised . . .'

'Do you think he will turn up?'

He rose to his feet and stood smiling down at me.

'Probably not.'

'Come then.'

Justin grasped me firmly by the elbow and steered me across the room. Our hostess was too engrossed to pay any attention to our going. Justin nodded good-night to some acquaintance as he passed. I found my wrap and we went out.

The air was cold even though the wind had fallen. The snow could not be far off. The lights shone clear and hard on the windswept pavement. No one seemed to be abroad. A sharp pain shot through my chest. I hunched my shoulders and wrapped my cloak more tightly round me.

Justin strode along with even, long-paced strides. In my high-heeled evening shoes I tripped along after him. I looked at him as he walked, his broad shoulders thrown back, his arms swinging slowly as if he were unaware of the cold. I began to laugh. He stopped and turned round.

'It is the same old Justin, always walking in front with his little dog trotting behind him.'

He slowed down his pace to suit mine and slipped his hand under my arm again. His hand was warm and strong.

'We'll pick up a taxi when we reach Holborn,' he said.

He was silent then. The only noise was the clatter of my heels and the firm sound of his as we walked along, except now and then the howl of a cat. Suddenly I became aware of the cats. The street was full of them. An enormous black and white tom cat sprawled in the middle of the roadway, spitting and growling at a grey tabby which was backing slowly away from him towards the footwalk. Then, with a sudden bound the black and white cat sprang forward, uttering the most heart-rending howls. The tabby turned tail and ran until she had gained the shelter of the gardens. There, from a bush, she spat defiance.

'I like the city at this time of night,' said my cousin. 'Mankind is asleep and the world belongs to the cats.'

WE found our taxi. It drew up in front of a high, barrack-like block of flats and three young men got out. They were in a merry mood and while two of them squabbled amiably with the taxi-driver, the third approached us. His hat was perched rakishly on the back of his head, his open coat showed his white shirtfront, marvellously stiff and white considering his condition. He tottered towards us, a silly smile on his face, his hand held out.

'Happy New Year!'

A sudden movement of Justin's hand warded him off. His face had the old keep-your-distance look. He did not reply to the greeting. At that moment, through the well-remembered gesture, the two Justins coalesced and I could see the lanky boy again in this strong, broad-shouldered man. I saw something else, too, his resemblance to our grandfather. I stepped behind him, as I had once been accustomed to do.

'No harm meant, I'm sure,' continued the young man. 'Why don't you come up and have a drink? Say — everyone come up and have a drink. All good fellows.'

'Get into the taxi, Loulie. No, no, sorry old man. We must be getting along.' Justin pulled open the door and pushed me in.

But the stranger was not so easily brushed aside.

He had arrived at that stage of intoxication when he felt isolated from humanity and was making despairing efforts to get close to his fellow-men.

'You don't like me. I can see you don't like me. Don't blame you. Nobody likes me. See those fellows there. They don't like me either. Here I am, this night of all nights, alone, without a friend, no one to take a drink with me, no one to hold out the hand of friendship. Now,' here he advanced again on Justin and laid his hand on the outstretched arm of my cousin. 'Now if you had one scrap of humanity in your heart, any love for your brother man, you would bear me company through the silent watches of the night, on this most auspicious occasion.'

Justin shook off the detaining hand and taking him by the shoulder pitched him forward towards his two companions who were still arguing with one another in a friendly way about the taxi fare. He gave the driver the address, climbed in beside me and banged the door.

'Shocking bore, a drunken man.'

'It's strange, Justin, to look at you now after all these years, so changed and yet so much the same.'

'Eh?'

'The way you always walked in front, the way you pushed that poor bloke off, the way your eyes darken when anyone touches you.'

'I never thought of it. I suppose it's true. I detest close contacts.'

As I sat huddled up in the corner of the cab, I watched my cousin's face as the street lights passed in bars across it. He sat slightly forward, his forearm on his knee, and looked straight before him. His lean face looked as if it had been cut out of some whitish stone. I felt myself in the presence of a stranger.

Justin's house was the house of a rich man. It stood, high and narrow, on the west side of an eighteenth-century square. The wintry branches of the trees in the gardens almost crossed the road, they were so old. We mounted the half-dozen steps and entered the house.

'Come into my den, it's warmer there. Do you remember grandfather's den, the high desk in the window and the row of walking-sticks?'

'And the bottle of whisky and the locked door and our terrors.'

'You remember how Aunt Molly used to lock us in and we crouched down under the blankets.'

'Long ago.'

'Those were happy days,' said my cousin. 'Come, let's drink to more happy days. What would you like?'

'What have you got?'

' 'Most everything.'

'Some sparkling wine?'

'Right you are.'

He returned in a few minutes with the tray.

I was examining the room when he entered. Though by no means versed in these matters it did not take me long to discover that everything in the room had cost a great deal of money.

'Justin, by what low means have you contrived to accumulate so much of this world's goods?'

'Sweat of my brow, girl. I am a lawyer.'

'A furred cat. Last thing I should have imagined.'

'Why not? It suits my particular nature very well.'

I looked at him again as he bent over the tray. What was his particular nature? I had not thought of it before. What was he really like, this cousin of mine? I felt I could have judged a stranger better.

'Busy?' I asked, taking my glass.

'Not just now. The flat racing season hasn't come on yet.' He grinned cheerfully at me.

'What's that got to do with it?'

'It's then the boys have the cash to hire a mouth-piece.'

'I see. It's funny, isn't it, we both live off the race-course. But why that side of the business?'

'Nothing gives me greater pleasure than turning a good criminal loose on society again. Drink up and have another glass and tell me what you have been doing all these years.'

'Newspaper work, marriage, roaming about.'

'Where have you roamed to?'

'To every racecourse in both hemispheres.'

'What?' My cousin looked at me in amazement.

'Oh, it's not as awful as it sounds. Egan is what is known as a professional punter. We have our ups and downs. He has sometimes even been reduced to working — but not often. However reckless he may be in the affairs of ordinary life, he is fairly cautious in the exercise of his profession.'

'I am beginning to think I shall like your husband. So you have been spending your life going places, while I have stayed here.'

'As grandfather used to say, I am like sherry, well-travelled.'

'Remember how we used to plan to sail round the world? It must have been fun.'

'Fun? You know how it is with sailors. They never see anything but the sea and sailor-town. The only things that change for them are drinks and the colour of the women. In my case it's been the race-tracks and the climate. The horses are always the same, the people the same and there is whisky wherever one goes.'

'You were homesick?'

'Often. Justin, you have only been telling me half the truth, the more romantic half probably. No honest burglar or set of burglars could supply you with these signs and tokens of wealth.'

'It is always easier to confess to a crime than to a misdemeanour. The fact is, Loulie, there are certain men in this world who make their money just within the law. They are in constant need of knowing just how close to the wind they can sail. That's what I'm for.'

'And they pay well.'

'Very well. But forget it. I am no more dishonest

in helping them to defraud society than the men are who support this society.'

'There was never man born who could not find a perfectly good reason for doing a bad thing, so I'll let it pass. We can argue it out some other time.'

'Tell me, Loulie, are you happy?'

'Who is? Are you?'

'No, I suppose not. But then I don't expect to be happy. Women always do. That's why they go on fighting.'

'They don't expect, Justin, they merely hope.'

'Hope,' cried my cousin, his eyes darkening. 'They drive the world mad with their hope — Oh, it would be such a lovely place — they cry — if you would but conform to our ideas, our ideas of your place and duties and obligations — Just like the Liberal Party.'

'They seem to be just about as successful.'

'Sure, and serve them right, say I. But we're not here to quarrel. Another drink? So we're not happy, Loulie? Well, who is?'

'Why should you be unhappy?'

'Who can be happy and free in this world?'

'You have so much.'

'Have I? Have you ever heard, little sobersides, that Satan is the Prince of this world? It's sound theology as well as sound common sense.'

I began to laugh.

'Well then, make a truce with him and don't try to dramatize yourself.'

'It is a national characteristic I value. Don't, for heaven's sake, become anglicized.'

He moved over and sat down beside me on the sofa.

'Do you know, Anne-Louise, you haven't changed such a hell of a lot after all? Now begin at the beginning and tell me all that has happened to you.'

'Too tired, Justin. Some other time, maybe.'

'Here, take off those ridiculous slippers and wriggle your toes.' He stooped down and jerked off my shoes.

'No, I'd better go home.'

'Why?'

'I want to sleep.'

'Sleep here. There's a room.'

I hesitated. I knew that Egan would not be home, yet I hoped that he would. I knew that I would lie awake waiting for him. I hugged my misery, would not be deprived of it.

'I must go home.'

Justin pushed me back and holding me by the shoulder looked straight into my eyes.

'If you must, you must. I'll see you back. But first, tell me why you must.'

'You know.'

'Anne-Louise Delahaie, what are you coming to? Like the little nightingale, you press your breast to the thorn — to sing all the sweeter, I suppose.'

'Get away, Justin.'

'Loulie, are you dragging your cousin out into the cold dark morning, just so that you can be miserable?'

'You needn't come. Ring for a taxi.'

'I needn't, but you know I will.'

'You are cruel, Justin.'

He threw back his head and laughed.

'It's always the way. When a man forces a woman to be truthful with herself, then he is cruel.'

'You are. You always were.'

'Are you staying?'

'I am staying.'

We went upstairs side by side, as we had done when we were children, quietly so that we should not wake Mrs. Barton, Justin's housekeeper. Just as he was about to show me into my room, he paused and crossed the landing to another door.

'Come here, Loulie,' he said. 'I want to show you something.'

He opened the door and I followed him into a large square room at the back of the house. I looked around me in astonishment. It was as if he had transported his old room from grandfather's house. There, its head to the wall, stood an old four-poster bed, a thick sheepskin rug on the carpet beside it. Square wooden chairs stood against the wall. High Queen Anne tallboys flanked each side of the fireplace and in front of the window was a long mahogany table. On the mantelshelf an old French clock by Bergeret of Paris ticked loudly and sharply and over

it hung a picture done in wools of Moses smashing
the Tables of the Law. I turned to my cousin.

'You brought them here?'

'No, only Moses. I picked up the bed in the
Caledonian market. But I felt I had to have Moses.
Do you mind?'

'Not a bit. I never particularly liked him. But
why, Justin?'

'I feel secure and happy when I sleep here. And
Moses, breaking the Tables of the Law, seemed
appropriate.'

From the transom of the bed came a furious
chatter. A small grey monkey looked down at us,
his bright, beady eyes blinking in the light and his
old wizened face creased and wrinkled with excitement.

'Here, Gringo. Come down and meet the lady.'

The little monkey slid down the bedpost and,
jumping into Justin's arms, climbed on to his
shoulder. There, its puny arms clasped round my
cousin's forehead, the little monster gazed down at
me, scolded and raged.

'Loulie, this is Gringo, specimen of Homo
Insipiens, and my very good friend. He's jealous
of you, my dear. He doesn't like ladies, do you,
Gringo? The sight of them puts him in a rage.
Now, be sensible, make friends with the pretty lady.
She's not like the others, she's my cousin.'

I shuddered.

'He's horrible, Justin. Take him away. I can't

199

bear monkeys. They are such caricatures of men, far too human to make pleasant company.'

'That's why I like them. Run along to your chair, Gringo. This pretty lady does not like you either.'

Gringo ran across the floor on all fours and jumped on one of the chairs. From there he continued his threatening chatter and shook his tiny fist at me.

'Come, I'll show you to your room.'

We walked across the landing again and into the other room. I glanced at it quickly. This was no man's room. It belonged to a woman, a young woman with elegant and conventional tastes. The lace bed-cover, the silk curtains, the soft thick carpet, the smell of the room, all these told of a female occupant.

'You'll find some night clothes in the chest over there, I think. Take what you want.'

'Thanks. Good-night, Justin.'

'Good-night, little cousin,' he smiled down at me. 'I'll leave a note for Mrs. Barton, telling her to wake you at midday. I'm glad I've found you again. Sleep well.'

In spite of the misery that gnawed almost continually at my heart nowadays, I slept. Falling asleep had become a struggle between my mind and my healthy body, for when Egan was not with me I was wondering where he was and with whom. My last waking thoughts were an agony, an agony which increased in intensity as my control over my senses vanished, and so great that it would often bring me full awake again. They were horrible, those moments before I became unconscious, moments of abject surrender to visions which in the day I could banish, moments which carried over into strange nightmares or sweet, confused, heart-breaking dreams of memory. Yet now I slept.

I awoke to the sound of curtains being drawn. When I opened my eyes, still heavy with sleep, I saw a plump, white-haired woman coming towards the bed. Her pink face was pleasant and smiling. On the table beside my bed stood a cup of tea. I took it gratefully.

'You are Mrs. Barton,' I said.

'Yes, Mrs. O'Doherty. I am very pleased to meet you. You are the only relative of Mr. Thorauld's who has ever been here.'

'Really? And it's a long time since he's seen me. We grew up together.'

'Mr. Thorauld asked me to send Jessie, the housemaid, for some of your clothes, Mrs. O'Doherty. It is very uncomfortable to have to go home in an evening dress. People stare at one so.'

'How nice of Justin to have thought of it.'

'He's a thoughtful person. Is there anyone there to let Jessie in?'

'I — I don't think so. I'll give you my key, it's over there in my bag.'

A second later Justin put his head round the door. His hair was wet after his bath and I thought how well and fresh he looked. I felt washed-out and sleepy.

'Ready for breakfast?' he asked.

'When I've had my tea and a bath.'

'Hurry up. What do you want to eat?'

'Nothing. Coffee, strong, lots of it.'

When I came into the dining-room, Justin was already there, going through his letters. His nasty little monkey was perched on the back of his chair, looking round with sharp malicious eyes, eyes that at the same time looked as sad as those of an old Jew. When he saw me he began chattering at me.

'Put that pest out of the room, Justin, or I'll have my breakfast with Mrs. Barton.'

'Keep quiet, Gringo. Why do you dislike him?'

'I loathe monkeys, as I told you already. Where did you get the horrid thing?'

'Sorry, Gringo, you'll have to go out. I picked him up, one winter's night, in the King's Road. The wretched little creature was sitting on the top of a barrel organ, too miserable to beg, or even scratch himself. His master did not look much better. So I bought the monk. You'll get used to him. Mrs. Barton almost gave notice when she saw him.'

He went back to his letters. I poured myself out another cup of coffee. Presently he raised his head.

'Sorry to be so absorbed but there's something rather annoying turned up. The way of the transgressor is hard. If you want a cigarette, there's some in the box at the end of the table.'

He read the letter through once again and then put it down.

'Been long in London?'

'About six months.'

'I wish you had looked me up.'.

'How?'

'Telephone book, girl.'

'Do you know, Justin, the look of the London Telephone Directory is absolutely terrifying to one unused to such marvels?'

'If my name were Smith I could understand.'

'Anyway, it never occurred to me. I've had a lot to occupy me. Tell me, Justin, have you married again?'

'No, why?' He began to laugh. 'My dear, if you had really examined the clothes in that chest you would have found they were three years out of date.'

'Why did you leave everything?'

'No one came to change it. How do you like London?'

'Loathsome. I'm afraid of everyone. It's a big cruel city.'

'Do you want to leave it?'

'If I could.'

'I'm afraid I'll have to go away somewhere for a while. Something has broken rather unpleasantly. Would you come with me?'

'And Egan?' I asked, and then could have bitten out my tongue.

'Sure. Just as you like.'

'Where shall we go?'

He leaned across the table, his head bent forward. The lock of hair fell forward across his forehead.

'Are you ever homesick, Loulie?'

'So that the bread tastes salt between my teeth.'

'We shall go home.'

WHEN I got back to my flat I found, as I had thought, that Egan had not yet come home. I wandered aimlessly from one room to another, tidying and rearranging, opening and shutting cupboards, sorting out the clothes I would take away from those I intended to throw out. I cooked myself scrappy meals and ate them standing at the kitchen table. Slowly the day went by, the early winter evening fell, but there was still no sign, no letter, no telephone call. I would not go out lest he should ring and yet in my heart I knew he would not. He never did.

The night passed, as many such nights had passed, in nightmare snatches of sleep. I did not switch off the light over my bed. If I did the first moments of waking were moments of terror. In the morning, weary of my own stupidity, I got up, determined to pack my bags and leave. But I was always obstinate. I could not bring myself to acknowledge defeat. I knew full well that Egan was slipping away from me, that I did not possess the wisdom to hold him, or if I possessed it, I could not use it. I knew that it would be better to leave him now than to watch him drift away, but I could not. There were times when I wished I could kill him to rid myself of this tyranny of love, yet I knew that even death would not set me free. It was a tyranny born as much in the mind as in the senses. I was caught up, like a rabbit in a snare, and I did not know which way to turn.

At three o'clock the telephone rang. I lifted the receiver with a trembling hand. It was Justin.

Had Egan come home? No, not yet. Or phoned? No. What was I going to do? I didn't know — wait.

'I want to get away to-morrow evening. I've wired Bella. If he's not back by then, leave your address.'

'I can't, Justin.'

'Don't be a fool, girl.'

'I'll ring you back to-morrow.'

Another day, another night. By midday I was angry, angry with myself. How long was I going to endure this? I walked up and down the room, clasping and unclasping my hands, watching the telephone as if it were alive, trying to bring myself to do something I had never done before. At last I went over to the table, lifted the receiver and slowly dialled a number.

'Hello! Is that you, Elizabeth? This is Louise O'Doherty speaking.'

There was no answer for a moment. I could almost see the hand passing over the mouthpiece at the other end.

'Oh, hello, Louise.'

'I've just rang up to say good-bye.'

'Good-bye? Really?'

'I'm leaving for Ireland this evening.'

'But how?'

'How? Oh, the usual way. In the train. Have

you seen Egan anywhere? I want to see him before I leave.'

'Egan? No, dear. I haven't seen him for more than a week.'

'Never mind. Good-bye.'

'Good-bye. Pleasant journey!'

I knew she was lying. She had seen him. He was probably in the room with her at that very moment. I telephoned Justin, who was out. I left a message. I went to the bank and cashed a cheque. When I came back, I packed my suit-cases, cooked a good meal and ate it. Then I wrote a letter to Egan, went round the flat to see that everything was in order, the gas turned off, the windows closed. I stopped for a moment in the little hall, took two five-pound notes from my bag and left them on the table beside the letter.

I HAD forgotten the winter, the bitter winter of the North, the harsh winds that bite to the very bone, the cruel frosts that lay bare the rock beneath the soil. I had forgotten the savage wildness of my country, a country in which nothing delicate can grow. Homesick, I had only remembered the soft west wind, the lush grass of summer meadows, the clear song of larks in the blue sky, the gentle murmuring water, the thousand smells and sounds of hot July days.

When I got out of the train at Derry, the wind caught me like a knife between the ribs, choked back the breath from my lungs. It pinched my hands and feet and set my teeth chattering. My city clothes were no protection against it. I stood on the platform, as miserable as Justin's little monkey, as incapable of movement. Gringo, wrapped in a rug, lay in a torpid condition at my feet. His eyes were dull and listless as if with pain. My cousin, his overcoat slung loosely across his shoulders, moved comfortably and quietly about, seeing to the luggage, and trying to find a taxi.

'In Iceland they have geysers,' I remarked as he pushed me into an ancient horse-cab, the only vehicle he had been able to discover.

'You'll be warm at the hotel. I'll have to leave you there and go down to the docks to see about the car. I hope it has arrived.'

'You might get me a thick sailor jersey, the kind the men wear at home, a heavy tweed coat and a pair of strong shoes.'

'Hadn't you better go yourself? I won't know the size.'

'I'll give you all the necessary details. I'm not stirring out until I am properly clad.'

As the cab jolted over the stone sets, I leaned forward and looked out at the ancient walled city of Derry, the first city I had ever seen. I had once imagined it a great city full of wonder and delight, the Baghdad of my fairy tales. Now it looked grey, dirty, shabby and small. Except for the hill on which the old town stands, it is built on piles and the mud oozes continually up into the street, especially here near the waterside. The houses which had once appeared so tall, now seemed dingy and low, the shops ill-lit and miserable. Men and women with still, dark, unhappy faces walked the streets. The slums of the bogside oozed out their wretched population as the streets did their mud. I wondered if all homecomings were like this. The bulls in Connaught have long horns. The far-off hills are green.

That night Justin and I sat in my room talking until the small hours of the morning. Rather, Justin talked and I listened. He spoke of his work, of his triumphs and defeats, and as I listened there came to my mind those nights in Dublin when I had sat, hugging my knees, listening to Egan. But Justin did not talk of women. He described the early years in London, just after the war, years of bitter struggle, until he fell in with a group of City men, ready to make use of his sharp wits.

'You may think it strange, Loulie, that I had few qualms of conscience. I don't think I had any. Poverty taught me to hate those who were exploited just as much as their exploiters. I enjoyed my work. It was fun pitting my brains against the law. One swindle against another, one swindler against the mightiest swindler of all. Justice, what had justice to do with it? The whole legal system is designed to protect the vested interests of society.'

'It would be better to try and change that.'

'Maybe. But why should I be a voice crying in the wilderness, a voice without power? I preferred to use it for my own ends, to make society give me all the good things it had to give, wealth, comfort, beauty. I got all I asked for and more.'

'You do not believe in justice?'

'There you're wrong, Loulie. I do. But is it justice that sends a boy or girl to a Borstal for some petty crime? Is it justice that punishes men and women for a disregard of the law of property when they have never had any property of their own? That sends a man to prison for having no visible means of support? The petty thief suffers and the company promoter escapes.'

'You are the one who helps him to escape.'

'Don't forget that, when I can, I help the thief to escape, too. I am no different from the others who earn their living in the smug practice of the law. I sometimes go a little farther than they do, that is all. Then, too, I have noticed a strange thing, Loulie. We Irish have this in common with the Jews, we do not seek to change the evil we find, we exploit it. It is as if we felt ourselves pushed outside the gates of respectability and uprightness by people no better than ourselves and consequently have no right to consider or be considered. The Jews and the Irish, they make the best shyster lawyers, the best gangsters of society—though we do not make the best criminals. We operate best within the law. Yet of all the peoples on earth, we have the deepest love of justice.'

'There was grandfather, Justin. What would he have said?'

'To be a just man, as our grandfather was, one must be born with money, or be content to remain poor and despised.'

'Are you satisfied?'

'The final test? I was, for a long time. As I said, I enjoyed it. I enjoyed living, too.'

'And then?'

'I don't know. For three years now, my life has seemed to have no more meaning than a game of chess. Suddenly a great emptiness came into it. Up to then so much had mattered to me, the satisfaction of my appetites, my sensual and intellectual pleasures, the joy of living, if you care to call it anything. Perhaps it was the death of youth. I can't say. One day it was there, the next gone.'

'And then?'

My cousin spread out his hands as if pushing away some invisible burden.

'Nothing. I went on. If the salt loseth its savour, wherewith can it be salted?'

'And now?'

'Now for the just man.' He stood up, laughed and stretched himself. 'Now for the years of contemplation.'

Gently he stroked my head.

'Go to sleep, little cousin. To-morrow night we shall be home.'

WE left Derry the following morning, as soon as Justin had made arrangements about taking the car across the border.

'May I drive?' I asked. 'I like driving and it's warmer.'

He moved over without protest.

'You probably know the way better than I do. Take the east road.'

'It's a bad road, especially this time of the year. It's eight miles longer, too. Better go through Inish.'

'No, I want to go home over the mountain.'

'On your own head be it if we are stranded on the side of Knockdhu, miles from anywhere.'

Ten miles out of Derry we left the main road. Here the aspect of the country changed at once and instead of pleasant farm lands a wild, desolate and barren landscape stretched out before us. Not so far as the eye could reach could be seen the white-washed walls of an isolated farmhouse, the smoke rising from a chimney. For miles on each side of the road the bog had been cut away so that it ran, a rough track, high over the surrounding country. Snow lay thick in the hollows and the bog-holes were frozen. Here and there small turf-stacks, left from the previous summer's cutting, showed like primitive dwellings, snow outlining the cracks on the windward side. On the far side of the bog the mountains rose, black against the wintry sky. A harsh wind blew from Scotland, cold and bitter, singing its whining song through the telegraph wires and whistling round the car. A land of Ossianic grandeur, cursed by a baleful eye.

As the road turned right to approach the Bull Pass, Justin said impatiently:

'Step on the gas, Loulie.'

'Daren't. She wouldn't hold the road and we'd go over the edge.'

'She'll hold it. Give her more gas.'

Reluctantly I pressed down the accelerator. The car rushed forward and then, meeting with a sudden outcrop of stone on the road, swerved round. I threw out the clutch, hoping the car would right itself. The rough surface of the road saved us but a tyre was ripped off. We got out to change it. While Justin stood contemplating the damage I went to the back of the car to get the jack. When I opened the door, Gringo, peering out from the folds of the rug in which he had been wrapped, whimpered pathetically at me. I felt sorry for the poor little creature, dragged up to this frozen land, to satisfy the whim of my cousin. A creature born in some country where the sun shone, how this little monkey must suffer when the cold north-east wind struck his frail body. I put out my hand and scratched his forehead. He put out his paw and seized my finger as a child does its mother's. He held it tight as if he would never let it go.

'Poor Gringo,' I said. 'We'll soon be home and there is a great fire there. Then you'll be warm again. Poor little beast!'

The whimpering ceased. He released my finger and closed his eyes. I left him and went to help Justin change the wheel.

'Shall I drive?' asked Justin.

'No. It's the only way I can keep warm.'

The car climbed slowly up to the pass. As we came near the top, Justin looked out through the window in the back and then turned excitedly to me:

'Loulie, back there. The Sea of Moyle. Do you remember once we rode up here to see it when we were children? We got caught in a storm.'

'I remember,' I answered, but I did not stop to look back.

'O'Cahan's house must be over there behind that hillock, if it is still there.'

'Very likely it is.'

When we had crossed the pass, and began to drop down on the other side, I drew the car in under the lee of a rock and we got out. Stretched out below us lay Glasthule Bay, winding and grey under a wintry sky, and far out the great bens faced the Atlantic. In the valley the fields were empty and on either side the great bog stretched away, a place of desolation, a blasted heath. We stood looking down on this scene, which we had cherished in our minds as sunny and warm, a place of shelter, and we were silent.

Bella was waiting for us. She was older. Her smooth black hair was iron grey and strong wrinkles appeared beside her eyes as they do beside the eyes of those who look long and searchingly out to sea. But her back was not bent. She stood as tall and strong as ever. The wind blew her petticoats against her stout legs as she stood in the doorway, her arms open to receive us.

'God bless ye, childer,' she cried as she kissed us. 'Ye were a long while in coming home.'

'We are cold, Bella,' called Justin. 'Where is the whisky?'

'Where would it be but in the master's office?'

While Bella bustled about, I looked around. This strong old house was my home, the only real home I had ever had. These strong walls could still protect me against the storm. The fire on the hearth still glowed and gave forth warmth and comfort. All was secure within, but the walls pressed more closely and the house was silent. It did not seem to answer the sound of our voices. They fell flat and dead against its walls. I moved over to the window and looked out on the cobbled yard. Grass grew between the stones. The horses were gone, the cows sold. A silence of death, of winter and old age, lay on the old homestead. Sighing I turned back into the house.

I wandered through the long corridors, entered the rooms one after the other. The cold struck through to my bones. I touched the walls. They were damp with the sea moisture. In the dining-room I stood and looked at the old portraits, at great-grandfather Thorauld with his lean wife beside him. Slowly I read the faded name on the frame: SUZANNE-MARIE-LOUISE TABUTEAUX, a long-nosed, tight-lipped woman, with gracious folded hands, resigned to what fate had sent her. I wondered had she loved my great-grandfather? Had they days and nights of joy in their lives? Or were their hours spent in the bitter accumulation of this world's goods?

Over the mantelpiece hung the portrait of my grandmother, whose christian name I bore, ANNE-LOUISE LEBLANC. As a child I had never noticed how lovely she was. Her dark red hair hung in ringlets on to her shoulders. She had a small oval face with grey eyes and arched brows. Her thin hands pressed her white dress against her slender body. Eagerly, expectantly she leaned forward.

I heard someone enter the room. It was my cousin. He came over and stood beside me.

'I never realized, Justin, how lovely she must have been. What a pity we did not know her.'

'No wonder grandfather stole her away,' said Justin softly. 'For such women young men go through fire and water.'

'I didn't know. Why did he steal her?'

'She was to have married his brother. Grand-father came home for the wedding. She fell in love with him and refused to marry our grand-uncle. She just took to her bed and like Ahab, refused to be comforted. Then her mother locked her in her room until she should come to her right mind. Grandfather climbed up there one night and took her out through the window. They ran away to this old house. She went with him eagerly enough. She was a woman who knew her own mind, and grandfather's too, probably.'

'What age was she then?'

'Sixteen. Grandfather was twenty-two. He had just come down from the university and was working for a fellowship.'

'Sixteen and twenty-two, they were children.'

'Do you remember the last time we met here? You were sixteen or a little more. I thought then: she is ripe for love. Was I right?'

I hesitated. What right had my cousin to know these things? Yet I answered:

'You were right.'

He moved away and from a shelf in the bookcase took down an old book, a copy of Tacitus. He opened it at the flyleaf and handed it to me:

'You didn't get the length of reading Tacitus, but I did. Look.'

There in my grandfather's fine handwriting were the words:

'Bought in Letterkenny on the twelfth day of June 1862, the day on which I first met Anne-Louise Leblanc.'

'I wonder,' I said, looking at my cousin, 'how long they loved one another?'

Justin smiled.

'Remember grandfather. Always, I should think. And now, all that is left of that old love is — you and me.'

Old books, old loves, dead as autumn leaves. I shivered. The old house was full of ghosts.

This was one of the wildest winters I could remember. For days on end we were forced to keep to the house because of the furious storms that tore down on the village. From the sea came news of wrecks, from inland tales of men and cattle lost on the mountains. Darkness fell early and lifted late and during the short hours of daylight few stirred abroad.

Neighbours began to call and farmers' wives from outlying farms when they came down to the village to buy stores. It was I, not Justin, who welcomed them and offered them hospitality. They brought presents to welcome us home, a fat hen, some eggs, a pat of butter. Some I remembered, but others had passed from my mind. The years had changed them. Bella never left me in any doubt as to who they were.

'Here's Mrs. MacSweeney of Knockglass come til see ye. Sit down, Mrs. MacSweeney, nearer the fire. You be to be perished on a day like yon. Tell us now, how is Maggie getting along in Derry? Does she like her new job at that school?' Then turning to me. 'You know Sara is married now on John Elkin of Carnduff and has two childer.'

So I was saved from making any awkward mistakes. I drank tea and chatted. I promised to go to the farm when the weather got better. I listened to stories of myself as a child and to stories of grandfather. Then they would go.

The day after our return Egan's mother came to see me. She brought me some duck eggs and Justin a pair of socks. Her fair hair had turned white now and her figure had shrunk. She had become an old woman, weary of life and the anxiety of children. She kissed me and stroked my hand.

'I'm glad til see ye again, daughter. Ye're welcome here.'

'Egan bid me give you his love,' I lied. 'He was busy and could not get away. Besides, he did not want to come until the bad weather is over. I came because I was homesick.'

She sighed gently.

'Och, aye, that's only natural. But it's a long while now since we've seen him. He be to be greatly changed.'

'Not much.'

'Now his wife's here, it's not likely he'll stay long behind.'

When she was going I said: 'Egan will be here in the spring.'

Did I say this to comfort her or because I wanted it to be so?

'He'll be needed. Hugh has more than he can rightly do.'

Old Manus was dead. Theresa, poor girl, had gone completely crazy. She wandered the roads, knowing no one, begging for pennies. As she was harmless she was left alone.

Wattie was now living with his sister Susan at the

other end of the village. Bella had no great opinion of Susan. She hinted that Wattie's present miserable condition was due largely to her lack of character.

'A poor creature,' she said severely. 'She makes no kind of attempt to control his habits, and ye know well what Wattie's habits are. And age mends few things. If I didn't go down there myself every once in a while, his state would be lamentable.'

'Why hasn't he been to see us?'

'He doesn't mind anything now from one day til the next. He hardly ever moves out. He's afeared, I think. It's a poor end for a man, squatting on his hunkers over a fire, meeting his Maker with speckled shins.'

On our way to visit him, Bella stopped us in the hall and took away the bottle of whisky Justin was slipping into his overcoat pocket.

'Give that here,' she said severely. 'A noggin's enough for him. Do you want to be the end of him?'

She went into the kitchen, filled out a half-pint bottle and brought it back.

'Take him that. It'll do him rightly.'

We found Wattie, as Bella had said, seated on a low stool, leaning over the fire. He glanced up when we came in, but he did not realize who we were. His sister, a kindly slut, hurriedly tucked the corner of her dirty apron into her waistband and then shook hands with us. She shouted across the room to Wattie:

'Wattie, do ye hear? It's the young master and

mistress come til see ye.' She pushed a chair over to the fire, unhooked her apron and dusted it. Carefully she replaced the corner of the apron. 'Sit down, Miss Loulie. Draw up til the fire. It's brave and cold the day. Wattie, Wattie, it's the young master and mistress.'

Wattie looked at us with bleary, red-rimmed eyes. Like so many old men he wore a hat and muffler and sat hunched up, his hands stretched out towards the turf fire.

'Aye so, aye so.' Then as if the sense of his sister's words had at last penetrated to his dulled wits he got up and stretched out his hand.

'Ye're welcome, indeed, ye're welcome. I'd have met ye at the station same as always, but they've sold the horses. They've sold the horses.' He shook his hand. 'More's the pity. I don't believe in them motors, indeed I don't. They won't last, I tell ye, they won't last.'

'We'll buy some more horses, Wattie,' I said, 'when the spring comes round.'

'Och aye, ye will surely.'

'You must come up to the house and have a look at them,' said Justin.

'I will, I will.' He cast a sly glance at his sister who was standing respectfully in the background and listening to every word. Then he lowered his voice to a hoarse whisper: 'If she'll let me.'

'Of course she'll let you,' said Justin.

Susan came forward and touched my shoulder.

'Don't heed him,' she whispered to me. 'He's strange now at times.'

'Ye'd wonder.' Wattie's hoarse whisper went on: 'She won't let me go a hen's race. She wouldn't let me out the other day when I wanted to go up to the house and bid ye welcome home. I ought to have been there, I know. I ought til have been standing there, to welcome ye back. And that other one's just as bad.' This was undoubtedly a reference to Bella.

'That's too bad,' said Justin. 'We missed you. See, I've brought you a present.' He took the bottle out of his pocket.

The old man's eyes lit up. He stretched out a trembling hand and seized it, uncorked it with one twist and pushed the neck into his mouth. He was about to swallow it in slow steady gulps when his sister dashed forward and snatched it from him.

'Have ye no manners?' she shouted. 'Can ye not offer the young master a drop?'

'No thanks,' said Justin. 'It's too early in the day for me.'

Susan took the cork from Wattie's trembling hand, drove it firmly into the neck of the bottle with the palm of her hand and then placed the bottle behind a plate on the dresser.

'We'd better be going,' I said, rising. 'Come over to the house next fine day, Wattie. We'll be looking out for you.'

Wattie hobbled to the door with us.

'I'll come,' he said, jerking his thumb slyly over

229

his shoulder. 'Some day I'll give her the slip, never fear. She's an awful woman, an awful woman. And so is the other.'

'Be sure you come,' said my cousin.

'As sure as Judgment Day.' The old man stood at the door nodding his head as we went across the green.

Justin seldom left the house. He had taken posses-
sion of grandfather's chair by the side of the fire,
where he sat for hours without speaking, reading the
well-thumbed volumes, a glass of whisky by his side.
Sometimes he would ask me to play a game of piquet
or chess with him. I never liked playing cards and
was an indifferent chess-player. I refused obstinately
all attempts to teach me. The king's bishop's gambit
always remained a dark mystery to me.

Often, of an evening, as I sat opposite my cousin,
I could not help wondering why he had so purposely
taken on the part of our grandfather. He possessed
nothing of grandfather's kindly tolerance, none of his
urbane goodwill towards men. There was in Justin's
bitter soul a dislike of his fellows which grandfather
had never known, an inverted idealism which grew,
not from his reason, but from his emotional nature.
Yet in every outward seeming he had become our
grandfather.

In the silence of the evening I would listen with
sharpened ears to the wind howling outside, rattling
the shutters and singing in the chimneys, to the far-
distant sound of heavy water breaking over the bar,
and my ancient terrors would return. The old house
creaked like a ship at sea. Strange rustling sounds
came from the wainscoting, the sighing of old
boards. On the other side of the wide hearth sat
my cousin, his dark thoughts hidden from all men.

By day I wandered through the overgrown garden where Aunt Molly's rose trees straggled over the walls, untended and unpruned, where the old apple trees stretched out their bare branches, torn and broken by the winds. I strayed through the stables, silent now, smelling of must and decay, through the empty, cobbled yards which rang no longer to the sound of the horses' irons or the jingle of harness.

A quiet despair had fastened in my heart. Every morning I waited with secret impatience for the letters to arrive. Every morning I took my mending to the window and sat there until the postman had passed. There was no letter from Egan. I invented a thousand small tasks to keep me busy. I sorted and arranged the books and made a list of those I intended to read. I cleaned and mended the samplers, overhauled the linen chests, made marmalade. I began to knit socks for Justin. As I said nothing, I thought my cousin noticed nothing.

One evening he laid aside the book he was reading and said:

'Have you heard from your husband, Loulie?'

The needle with which I was sewing ran into my finger.

'No.'

'Isn't your patience nearly at an end?'

'I am very patient.'

'No, you're not, you're just obstinate. As thran as they're made. Tell me, what are you going to do?'

'Nothing.'

'Just nothing. You plan to sit down every morning by the window until the postman has passed. You intend to sit here every evening, your ears strained for a knock on the door. Waiting, waiting, for what?'

'I don't know.'

'Do you think your husband will divorce you?'

'No — no. Why should he?'

'He may have more sense than you. When a marriage is over, it should be broken.'

For a moment I hated Justin for speaking what I knew to be the truth.

'Is it over?'

Justin shrugged his shoulders.

'I'm asking you, my dear.'

I had no answer. My cousin came over, caught my shoulders and gently shook me.

'Where's your pride, girl? You know there's only two ways open before you. Either you go out alone into the world or you stay here with me. Do you know what it will mean if you stay here? Peace, understanding, love. Do you hear, Loulie? This old home, our home, can shelter us against all the storms, as it sheltered our grandfather.'

'It's running away, Justin.'

'From what? No, my dear, it would be running away if you left me now.'

I pushed back the hair from his forehead.

'Times are changing, Loulie. Wherever we go, we are lone wolves, outcasts. In England because we are Irish. The English hunt in a close pack. Here in Ireland because we do not belong to the people. We are thrown out by both sides. We no longer have any power. We no longer serve any purpose. We are an unhappy race, nothing is left us but our personal life and our emotions. Don't I know why you married as you did? It was an instinctive desire to establish yourself securely, to leave a sinking ship. Oh, I don't blame you. It would have been wise if it had worked. But in your case it didn't.'

'We can take our place with the others, Justin, work with them, live with them.'

'No, dear heart, we can't because they won't let us. It is not what we are but what we represent that separates us from them. Has your husband never once turned on you, reminded you of who you are?'

'Yes — often. But he is not the whole country. There are many who have gone over.'

'Only a few, for the most part women. They have turned their coats, adopted a strange faith, denied their own, but how far have they gone? They must still feel the almost insuperable barrier raised up against them.'

'It may be our own fault.'

'It's no one's fault. We must accept circumstances. If we are to die out, let's step aside and die as the creatures do, without complaint or fuss. We have one another.'

'What would you have me do, Justin?'

'Stay here with me, live with me until death comes to seize us by the hair.'

'But why, Justin, why?'

'Little cousin, little stupid, can't you understand? I love you. There will be peace in your arms.'

His voice was low, his dark eyes soft and loving and eager. I bent forward and kissed him.

That evening Egan came home. He walked into the sitting-room slowly as if he were reluctant to be there. He stood before me without speaking, his wet clothes dripping on to the rug. Slowly he unfastened each button of his coat with the deliberate gesture of a sleep-walker. His eyes, bloodshot and strained, looked out far, through the walls of the house, as if he were gazing at some distant horizon. He did not answer my greeting, but throwing himself down in a chair, buried his face in his hands. I spoke to him again, but his only reply was a moan.

'You are wet through. Don't you think you'd better take off your coat?' My voice was harsh with pain and anger.

Still there was no reply.

'Where in God's name have you been all these weeks? What have you been doing?' I cried, though I knew it would be far wiser to leave him alone. But anything was better than this grim silence.

'Don't bother me.' His voice was dull and heavy. 'Do you think I want to remember?'

I felt that I wanted to weep but could not. I

wished someone would strike me, hurt me, so that I could shed the tears which lay as heavily on my soul as death.

I went out to the kitchen to get him something to eat. Justin was there, talking to Bella. I had the feeling of having interrupted two conspirators.

'Is there any broth in the pot, Bella?' I asked.

'Better give him some whisky,' said Justin. 'It's a bad day for walking.'

'From the clabber he's been shedding all over my clean hall,' Bella remarked, 'he would seem to have travelled all the roads of Ireland. Aye, ye can have some broth.'

She ladled it into a bowl and gave it to me.

When I returned to the room, Egan was still sitting where I had left him. The heat of the fire was raising steam from his clothes and boots. He raised his head and looked at me. I put down the bowl of soup on the table, crossed the room and laid my hand on his head. He took my other hand in his, my left hand, and with his clumsy fingers began to turn the wedding ring round and round on my finger. He smiled at me. My heart was breaking. Could he not see that my heart was breaking? He pulled me down beside him and held my head close to his.

'Sit over and eat your soup,' I said. ''Twill do you good.'

'Little Brer Rabbit? Just lays low and ses nuffin.'

'Egan! My dear, my dear!' I buried my head in his shoulder.

'There's nothing I can say, sweet, nothing. You know what I am like. You should never have married me. I'm not fit to be married.'

'I love you,' was all I could say.

'I know, I know,' he said impatiently. 'But love is never enough. I love you, too, but does that stop me from making a fool of myself? Does it stop me from drinking, wasting money and running after other women? You should throw me out.'

Was he trying to drive me away? — I thought. I could not let the matter rest.

'Do you want me to send you away?' I asked.

'No, no.' He waved his hand impatiently.

'What do you want, Egan?'

'If I only knew, dear, it would all be so easy. Lou, I know it's been hard all this time.'

I could not bear this, least of all from Egan. I covered his mouth with my hand to stop him. But he continued:

'Yes, yes, I could see it, in spite of your accursed pride. Do you know that pride is one of the seven deadly sins? Do you know that Lucifer, son of the morning, fell through pride? You are one of his fallen angels, dear, fallen, fallen, so low.'

'Don't talk of it,' I implored.

'There you go. Why don't you speak out, curse me, drive me away?'

'You know why.'

'Little one, there is a demon that gnaws at my heart, that drives me on from one place to another, from one woman to another. Have patience. Some day he will weary and I shall be at peace.'

'I knew that when I went away with you. And I have been happy, too.'

'Have you? It's strange, I haven't. I have never been happy.'

'Don't say that. It's a lie. Don't say it even to make me unhappy. I am happy when you smile at me.'

He threw back his head and laughed gaily, carefree.

'Sweet, you are the loveliest liar in the world. Come, I'm hungry. I want my broth.'

He moved his chair over to the table and began to eat holding my hand in his free one.

'Lou,' he said. 'It will be different now, you'll see. Now we've come home again, back here where we belong, back here to the North, everything will be changed. We've left the foul dunghill of humanity behind and come back among our own people. Great people, aren't they? Lou, my white love, you'll never be sorry again. Don't leave me again, girl, promise me, you'll not leave me.'

I was happy. For again I was deceived, again I deceived myself, once again I thought it had been our surroundings, our circumstances which had been at fault and not ourselves.

The door opened and my cousin Justin entered the room, a couple of glasses in one hand and a bottle under his arm. He placed the bottle on the table, holding the neck in his hand and turning the label towards Egan.

'You're welcome home, O'Doherty. How do you find Loulie? She's looking well, isn't she? See, I've brought out one of our grandfather's bottles of whisky. Persse's. There aren't fifty left in the world. It must have irked the old man to die and leave them behind.'

Egan stretched out his hand towards the glass.

'Your health,' he said to my cousin. Then turning to me, 'Your happiness, Lou.'

I looked at Justin. His eyes were laughing. Why was he laughing at me?

At first I was happy, happier than I had been for years. Here in our native village where distractions were few, Egan again became my love of the early days. He laughed at me, teased me, followed me around, invented fantastic stories to amuse me. He refused to go out without me. When the weather was fine we wandered around the countryside together, clambered along the rocky seashore, gazed down into the deep rock-pools where the sea anemones closed their tendrils over the grains of sand we dropped down on them. For hours we would watch the gannets fishing off the bens, dropping sharply from the air as they folded their wings to dive. We talked to everyone we met. As we tramped the roads, each mountain, each valley called forth some tale I had never heard, never could have heard, a folklore

in which fantasy and realism were curiously blended.
I began to know the country and the people as I had
never known them. My cousin never came with us.

It was Bella who introduced the first note of dis-
cord. She showed by every act that she disapproved
of Egan's presence in the house. To her I was the
young mistress and Justin the young master. Egan
had no business to be with us. He should have
stayed where he belonged, on his father's farm. Her
animosity took strange forms. She would not hear
what he said. She forgot to have his shoes polished.
She sent his laundry home to his mother until the
day when I discovered this and threatened to do it
myself. She even went so far as to hope that he
would die young. One day she said to me:

'He'll go the way his sister Hanna went, of a
consumption.'

'God forbid,' I answered, alarmed at her bitterness.

'You'll see,' she said grimly. 'He has the same
look in his eyes. He'll hurry it on with the drink.'

'Bella!' I cried. 'You have no call to say such
things. It's wrong to wish anyone evil.'

'I wish him no evil. He'll bring that on himself,
and pray God he does not bring it on mine as well.'

However great Bella's dislike of Egan might be,
it was nothing compared with her hatred of Justin's
monkey. If she met Gringo suddenly on the stairs
or in one of the rooms, she would scream and draw
her skirts about her as some women do when they

see a mouse. She couldn't bear to stay alone in the room where he was. Gringo seemed to like her, or to like tormenting her, for he followed her into the kitchen whenever he got a chance. Probably he associated her with the onion basket. Sometimes he would pick up her wide petticoats and slip underneath. When she moved he ran along after her, nothing but his tail showing. When he was discovered, the potstick would descend on his hind quarters and he would be driven out of the kitchen with curses. Gringo hated Egan. When Egan came near him, the little monkey raged and fumed with spite and fury. Egan had the countryman's contempt for all animals which could not be put to some practical use.

Then one day when Egan and I were tramping up the mountain road towards Knockdhu, we met a young woman. She came walking towards us with a light, swinging step, her petticoats fluttering in the wind. Her dark face, framed by the black shawl, was lit up by wide grey eyes, eyes that with their Mongolian slant seemed to mock the whole world. One of the mountainy people, I thought, and was about to pass on with a good-day. Suddenly she wheeled round and drew up before us with a gay, dancing step.

'Egan O'Doherty,' she cried in Gaelic. 'God be with you.'

I knew no Gaelic, just the few words and phrases I had learned as a child from Bella. But part of that conversation I understood.

'My wife,' Egan replied in the same tongue, nodding in my direction.

She held out her hand to me.

'God be with you!' she said.

'God and Mary with you!' I replied.

She looked me over from head to foot as if I were a strange being from another world.

'Ah! You understand Gaelic?'

'No!' I answered.

She turned again to Egan and said something I could not follow. They stood talking for a while in the bantering tones that country people use when they are not completely at ease with one another. Presently she looked at me again and asked Egan:

'How many children have you?'

'None,' he answered.

Her eyes danced in her head with malice and joy. Her white teeth gleamed between her full, red lips.

'None? Think shame on yourself, man. I wouldn't mind but she's a pretty girl.'

Egan laughed and then leaning forward slightly he spoke. I did not understand a word of what he was saying. The laughter died out of the girl's grey eyes. Her wide face became first blank, then red with anger.

'The devil!' she said and spat on the road.

She threw her arms out wide and gathered her shawl close around her, turned and hurried down the hill.

'Who is she?' I asked.

'Kate Sweeney of Carrabeg,' said Egan. 'I went to school with her.'

I said no more but I was uneasy. For the first time since his return Egan looked gloomy and distant. He could never endure to be treated slightingly by a woman. I asked myself what grudge the girl bore him that she should insult him in this primitive way. Even here the old shadow fell on me. All that evening Egan was silent and gloomy.

The following day when I went to fetch him, I found him playing chess with Justin. He glanced up when I came into the room and then continued the game without speaking.

'Your queen's in check,' I laughed, leaning on the back of his chair.

'What are you talking about?' said Egan. 'There's my queen.' He put a finger on the piece in question.

Justin looked up and grinned.

'Never fear,' he answered. 'I'll take her sooner or later.'

I did not see the end of the game.

From this time a strange friendship grew up between my husband and my cousin. There is nothing so disquieting to women as the secret companionship of men. There is no equivalent in their lives. It seemed to me that I was only admitted to their company on sufferance and that only in the beginning. Gradually, imperceptibly, I was completely excluded.

Sometimes they took the car and disappeared together for days. When they came back they never mentioned where they had been or what they had been doing. Justin was as reticent as Egan. Indeed they spoke very little during the day. For hours they would sit opposite one another in almost complete silence, playing one game of chess after another.

Night after night the bottles were placed on the dining-room table. Night after night they drank, and as the whisky loosened their tongues they talked and sang until the small hours of the morning. Yet no matter what they talked of, in the end they came round to the same subject, the war. It lay always at the back of their minds, a dark dream, only released when the fumes of alcohol rose to their heads. Night after night I lay in bed and listened. Through the old house rose their disputes, their laughter, the sound of voices as they sang:

'We fought at Mons and at Landrissy,
  On the Marne . . .'

I was troubled and unhappy, not because Egan was drinking, but because there was some link between him and my cousin which I could not understand and which I hated.

As the weeks passed the weather began slowly to change. The lull between the storms became longer and with the lengthening of the days life stirred in the valley. Long before the first leaf showed, first the thrush, then the blackbird shouted, sang and boasted from dawn to dark, and from high in the clear air came the shrill note of the lark. Men moved about the fields. The spring planting began. Every one was busy, everyone going somewhere. There was an air of hurried activity, of happy endeavour as if man had not the time to do all that he wished to do. The voices of women, the whistling of young men, the gay laughter of children rang in our ears. Spring, the eternal resurrection, had come again to make glad the heart of man.

But the old house remained as gloomy as ever. The dark panelled walls, the long corridors refused to catch the light. The high grey walls cut us off, as they had cut off my cousin and me when we were children from the life which flowed around us. We were apart from all that was going on.

It was wrong; I felt it was wrong to drag on this existence behind high walls. Our lives should be joined with those of our fellow-men. We should take part in their labour. When I suggested to Egan and Justin that we ought to re-stock the farm and plant the garden and fields, Justin refused. He had no desire to turn farmer.

'We are neither landlord nor peasants,' he replied. 'We are one of the oldest bourgeoisies in the world. Like all merchants, we have no feeling for the earth.'

'It would give you something to do.'

'It would. But do I want something to do? I prefer a life of contemplation.'

'Don't try to excuse yourself. You are just lazy.'

'My dear Loulie, you have a nasty belief, shared by so many women, that man must be made to labour. I know quite well that in your opinion we are superfluous, necessary only for the act of procreation. But is that any reason why I should be chained to a plough?'

There was no arguing with him. I turned to Egan.

'Do what you like,' was his surly reply. 'It's not my land. I have no interest in it.'

I suppressed the retort that rose to my lips. It would answer no purpose to antagonize Egan further. He was becoming very restless and discontented. Constant drinking was making him ill-tempered. I noticed that he was moving away from my cousin. He went home to his father's house more frequently, went fishing at times and talked with the men in the village. He was being drawn back into the life that went on outside the grey walls, a life to which by tradition at least he belonged. One day while I was working in the garden he came to me. I looked up from the seed-bed I was making to see him frowning at me.

'I'm leaving here,' he announced abruptly.

My heart sank. Was the eternal wandering to begin again?

'Why? Where?' I asked.

'I'm going home for a while. I can't bear this damned house any longer. It's giving me the jim-jams, I tell you.'

'Shall I come along?'

He lost his temper.

'Can I never be alone?' he asked in a furious, excited tone. 'Why must you follow me everywhere? Leave me be, for God's sake. I want to get away from this place and all in it. You're like your cousin, you would eat me alive.'

Justin did not seem to notice Egan's departure. At any rate, he said nothing about it to me nor did he go up to the farm to see him. In the evenings he sat alone in the dining-room, reading, working out some game of chess and drinking. He did not desire my company or he would have sought it. He scarcely noticed my presence in the house. He was quieter than before and seldom moved out. He became morose and spoke little. Even Bella began to treat him with restraint. She never approached him directly now, but through me.

'Ask the young master . . .' she would say.

Now that spring was here, Wattie remembered his promise to come and visit us. One morning I went into the kitchen and found him sitting close up to the fire. He presented a strange sight. Aunt Molly must have given him grandfather's clothes

247

and now he had donned them to pay us this visit. They hung on his shrivelled, bent body like rags on a broomstick. Grandfather's silk hat, kept obviously for funerals and weddings and such occasions as this, covered his unkempt, grey hair.

Bella was shouting at him as some shout at the old and deaf. He appeared to be paying little attention to what she was saying. From time to time, he lifted one claw-like hand from his knee, fluttered it gently to and fro before letting it drop back again.

'Will ye houl' yer whisht, woman,' he muttered peevishly. 'Ye'll deave me wi' yer clatter. Ye've a tongue the length of to-day and to-morrow.'

'But I tell ye, man, there's no horses.'

'No horses? No horses? Didn't the young master himself invite me? Wattie, ses he, come up til the house some day and have a look at the horses. Now, put that in your pipe and smoke it.'

'The man's daft, clean daft,' said Bella, casting her eyes up to heaven. 'What would he be doin' wi' horses when he has a motor.'

'I don't hold wi' motors,' said Wattie. 'They go runnin' here and runnin' there and duntin' intil people and knockin' them down.'

'I'm glad you've come to see us, Wattie,' I said. 'I'll go and fetch Justin.'

'Who's yon?' he asked, nodding towards me as I left the room.

'Who promised him horses, anyway?' Justin asked without looking up from his book.

'We both did.'

'All right. I'll be along in a minute. Give him a drink.'

I took the decanter from the sideboard and went back to the kitchen where Bella and Wattie were still arguing.

'Horses? Horses? 'Tis of yer latter end ye should be thinkin' and not of horses.'

'I can make my peace wi' Almighty God wi'out yer help, Bella. I came because I was asked.'

'Of course you did, Wattie, and we're very glad to see you,' I said.

'You've growed a big girl, Miss Loulie.'

'Haven't I, Wattie? Here's a drink for you. Justin will be here in a minute.'

'Thank you, Miss Loulie, and your very good health. It's grand — I was only this minute saying it to Bella here — it's grand to see you back in the old house. It hasn't been the same this long while since the old master went. It was a bad day for Wattie when they carried him out of here feet foremost, a bad day. Petticoat rule, ever since then, nothing but petticoat rule. It's a hard thing for a man to end his days, dragooned, pushed about and blackguarded by a pack of women.'

'We all mean kindly by you, Wattie.'

'Maybe you do. Still, it's a great satisfaction to me that there's a master in the house again. But tell me, Miss Loulie, where's the other one?'

'What other one, Wattie?'

'Och, ye mind. The lovely young lady that was married on the young master.'

'She's dead.'

Wattie shook his head sadly.

'Dead, did ye say, dead? That's terrible. She was a good girl, good to old Wattie. They all die except Wattie. What was it killed her?'

What killed her? A bullet. My heart beat thick and fast in my throat. I had forgotten all about Nell, forgotten that she had been Justin's wife, forgotten the whole sorry story. A hand was laid on my shoulder. My cousin had come into the kitchen so quietly that I had not heard him. I did not dare look round.

'I don't know, Wattie. I was not there.'

'Maybe she was delicate.' The old man lifted a hand and rubbed his scrubby chin. 'God rest her soul!'

'So you've come to see me about the horses, Wattie? You know the fair isn't for another fortnight. Maybe you'll come with me, if I go.'

'I might,' Wattie answered. 'If I'm let.'

Not since the days of the fighting in Dublin had I known such fear. It stayed with me day and night, wandering through my dreams and thoughts like water through sand. Fear grew beyond reason, beyond all stifling. Even by day it did not leave me alone but drove me to frenzied activity. I worked in the garden until I was dropping asleep from exhaustion, but when I lay down sleep was more terrible than waking.

I found myself examining my fear as a man examines his debts, wondering how they can be paid off, or forgotten. It was useless to say to myself that Justin could have learned nothing from those few words I had spoken to Wattie, useless to repeat that he had not loved his wife nor cared what had happened to her. I knew too well the ruthlessness of his character.

Old dreams, which had haunted me years ago, emerged triumphant from their hiding-places. Again I saw those black, uniformed figures leaping from their lorries. Again I heard the crackle of revolver fire, the rattle of machine-guns, the explosion of bombs. I stood at a street-corner with Tom Hennessy who whispered: 'Ellis came over to-night. They will hang him in the morning. No hope now. Pray for his soul. Pray for his dark, unhappy soul.' Justin sat high above me on a bench, a judge in robes and wig. He pointed beyond me and cried: 'Thou shalt not kill!' He put on the black cap —

the kibosh — the cap of death. I screamed: 'There was an amnesty, Justin! There was an amnesty!' Then he looked straight at me, his dark hair falling over his forehead from beneath the wig. 'There is no amnesty for the soul.' I awoke strangled with sobs.

I became stupid and childish with fear. I scarcely spoke to Justin or replied to his questions. When he said something to me, I trembled. I was afraid that I would accidently say something which would betray me. I spent my evenings alone in my room and watched the door, dreading his entrance. He never came. He did not question me. He was unfailingly kind and gentle, yet my terror did not decrease. For the first time in my life I longed for a mother to whom I could pour out my heart, the whole burden of my fearful thoughts.

I wanted to run away but I could not go. My fear held me fast as with fetters. I must be here when Egan came back. I was sure that he would come back and I hoped that I might save him. Save him from what? I had no idea.

Then I thought — if I can get Egan to come away with me, we shall both be safe. But what should I tell him? Never since that day in Stephen's Green when I had begged him to spare Nell, had I mentioned her name. How could I do it now? I must find some other reason, my health, lack of money, anything. But I must not mention my fear.

I set out to find him. He was not at the farm. His mother sighed as she replied to my question:

'We haven't seen hilt nor hair of him this week past. He be to be staying somewhere up the glen.'

'Where is Hugh?' I asked.

'In the Barra field.'

I went there to find Hugh top-dressing the pasture. He was a spare man with heavy bones and a rigid unsmiling face, burned red by wind and weather.

'He hasn't been home this good while,' he answered.

'Have you no notion where he is?'

Hugh stood looking far out towards the western sky, his grey eyes empty of all expression.

'I don't know,' he said slowly. 'But I've heard tell that he's beyond at Carrabeg, helping Matthew Sweeney. I could do rightly wi' a helpin' hand here. He was always an unchancey mortal.'

My heart sank in my breast like a stone. A girl with a light step and swinging skirts, a dark face with slanting grey eyes and full red lips.

As I entered the house I met Justin.

'I'm going to see Aunt Molly,' I said. 'It's high time one of us went. We are an ungrateful crew.'

'Good!' he answered smiling. 'Would you like the car?'

I was half-way to Derry when I changed my mind. I turned the car and drove back. Why had I not thought of it? I asked myself. Justin had let me go so easily, had offered me the car, too, so that he should be alone with Egan. I was a fool. I must get back.

I got home before nightfall. Save for Bella, the house was empty. The village girl who helped her had gone home and Justin was nowhere to be seen.

'Where's everybody?' I asked Bella.

'If you mean the young master. He left the house just after you and I haven't seen sight nor sign of him since. He hasn't been back for his meal and he knows rightly that it goes to my heart to see good food wasted.'

I sat down by the kitchen fire.

'Is there any broth, Bella?' I asked.

'Sure there is, my lamb. I'll give ye a good bowlful. Ye be to be starved after that long drive.'

'Don't you find this house lonesome when there is no one in it, Bella? If I had realized it I would never have asked you to stay.'

'Where else would I go, alanna? This has always been my home. I could not accustom myself to strangers at my age. It was best to stay.'

'Why did you never marry?'

She paused for a moment before answering.

'I suppose if the truth be told, it was because nobody ever asked me, and maybe, too, because I never looked for it. I've always had a poor opinion of men. At the best they're foolish and at the worst they make trouble. There's no comfort to be got from them either way.'

'I wish Justin had married again. Whatever you may say, Bella, Holy Writ has it that it's not good for a man to live alone.'

'I'm not saying what's good for a man but what's good for a woman. Do you know what happened to his wife, alanna?'

I felt an urgent need to talk, to share the burden of my thought with someone. After all, Bella was nearer to me than anyone else.

'She was shot in Dublin during the trouble.'

'We heard nothing of it. Was it in the paper?'

'It was, but I managed to keep Justin's name out of it.'

'Why was she shot?'

'She was employed by the British authorities as an agent, a person who went about and got hold of the boys who were fighting and found out things.'

'She deserved what she got, God forgive her.'

'I suppose she did. I was very sorry, for I liked her. But the worst of it was — I know who did it.' I could not tell the whole truth. It was too hard and bitter.

'My lamb!' said Bella. 'Don't fret yourself.'

'I don't want Justin to know.'

'Don't be troubled, child. Only the Almighty can read our hearts. Take comfort. When we are old we can sit by the fireside and laugh at the things that broke our hearts when we were young.'

I began to cry, to weep my heart out as I had done when a child. To sink back into childhood against Bella's broad shoulder, to imagine that I was grieved for the loss of some pet animal or toy, brought solace to my heart. I was comforted.

AT eleven o'clock there was still no sign of Justin. I left a note on the hall table to say that I had come back, went to bed and presently fell asleep.

I could not have slept long when I was awakened by voices. I sat up in bed and put my hand out for the matches. I lit the lamp and looked around me. The fire was burning low in the grate and beside it lay Gringo, curled up asleep. He had been lonely and sneaked into my room. I went to the door and listened. Downstairs in the hall, Justin and Egan were talking. From their loud tones I guessed that they had both been drinking. I wondered if I should go down or wait until morning, hoping wildly all the while that Egan would come up to me. I decided to stay where I was. On my way back to bed I threw a shawl over the little monkey and put a couple of turf sods on the fire to keep him warm.

I heard them coming up the stairs and my heart beat so that it choked me.

'Loulie, are you awake?' It was Justin's voice.

'Yes, yes,' I answered. 'But I am in bed.'

'Mind if we come in? We want to talk to you.'

'Yes, yes. Come in.'

Egan came over and kissed me.

'Little Brer Rabbit,' he said. 'You look lost in that great bed. Sweet little Brer Rabbit, always so good and gentle, isn't she, Justin? Always loving and kind. She's so clever, Justin, she just lays low and ses nuffin. She's unique, the only woman in the world who can say nothing.'

Dear God! They were both terribly drunk.

'She's a dangerous woman,' said my cousin. 'Foolish women talk, but she's like a clam, silent as an oyster, secret as the grave. Must give you a feeling of power, little cousin, to have secrets. To know things and not tell them. Marvellous, isn't it? Some day when you are old and you hear Death knocking at your door, you'll cry loud into the night: "One moment, kind Death, I have not told my secrets," and what will Death answer? "You can tell them to me, your last lover. The night is long when we shall lie together and you can tell them to me, every one, and I shall listen." '

Justin's head bent forward and the unruly lock of hair, so carefully brushed back, fell forward, shading his left eye. He pushed it back impatiently but it fell forward again. The years seemed to have dropped from him. He looked as he had done when he was a little boy. His face had a kind of unearthly beauty and his eyes, of a blue that is almost black, shone in the dull lamplight.

'Pay no heed to his miserable moan,' cried Egan, bringing his hand down heavily on my knees. 'If Death is your last lover, sweet, he is a discerning lover. He will not take you until you are ready for him. Where's the drink, Justin?'

Justin took two bottles from his overcoat pocket

and placed them on the table. He leaned against the side of the bed.

'No glasses. We must have glasses. Three. We must give Loulie a drink.'

'I'll get them,' said Egan leaving the room.

'Do you mind doing your drinking in some other room?' I said sharply to my cousin. 'There are plenty and I would like to sleep.'

'You would like to sleep, Miss Honeyball? But can you? When the mind is in torment, does the body sleep?'

'Leave me,' I cried. 'Leave me be.'

'I have it in my mind, dear, that this is the last night we three shall spend together. Why I should think so, I do not know. But to-night, I refuse to deny myself the sight of you. I want to sit here and watch you.'

His intensity, the dark glitter of his eyes frightened me.

'Go away. You are loathsome!'

'SO!' he whistled. Then he went to the door and shouted:

'Don't forget the corkscrew.'

Justin piled more sods on the fire. I sat up in bed, reached for my dressing-gown and wrapped it round me. I could see that further argument was useless.

'I am drunk,' said Egan, as he came back into the room. 'I am very drunk. I have not been so drunk in years. Divinely drunk.'

'Here, have another drink,' said Justin. 'When

one is drunk, there is nothing to be done but get more drunk. We must go forward. There is no turning back on this road.'

'We must go all the way,' said Egan, pouring the whisky into a tumbler.

'What have you both been doing?' I asked.

'We wished to be as gods, knowing neither good nor evil,' said my cousin.

Egan sat down on a stool by the hearth and Justin in a low chair by the table. Neither looked at me.

'The first time I aspired to godlihood in contradistinction to godliness was when I was up at Oxford,' my cousin continued. 'I cannot say that it was a pleasant experience or a memory I cherish. A lot of noise, wild talk, a girl in an alleyway and a terrible hangover the next day. I had not yet got my sea legs. I didn't get them until I joined the army.'

'I learned to drink in France,' said Egan. 'I had an officer there, name of Falconi. He was born in England of an Italian father and an American mother. My God, he was handsome. He was the most beautiful man I have ever seen. He was rich, too. He had his horses brought out to France and kept them back of the lines, and his women, too. I never could decide in those days which looked the better, the women or the horses. Now I know. No woman is as beautiful as a horse. Have you ever seen a woman who was as beautiful as a horse?'

'Yes,' Justin answered. 'But only once.'

'He gave me a bottle of whisky every day. I was

with him when he died. We were in a shell-hole and he was writing a dispatch, when they got him, straight in the kidneys. He held out his hand with the paper and said: "I've got a packet, O'Doherty". I took the dispatch. He was dead. I ran and as I ran I cried. I have never cried like that over a woman.'

'I remember once coming back from the front line,' said Justin, slowly. 'At that time I thought I was hard. I had seen so much and felt so much that I did not think there was anything that could touch me again. We passed a dead man. He had been wounded in the groin and had unfastened his trousers to examine the wound when he fell back, dead. Some-one had covered his face. And as I looked I thought, that part of him which he had kept covered when in life, is exposed, and his face, which all his life was naked, is now covered. I felt sick. That night I got very drunk.'

As my cousin spoke his head fell forward, his long thin hand shot out. The fingers groped along the edge of the table until they found his glass.

'Once,' said Egan, 'we were in a French village, for the love of me I can't remember the name. Maybe its name's gone up in smoke like so much else. But people still lived there. We robbed the quartermaster's stores to get money for drink. There were twelve of us. We found a pile of kilts for the Gordon Highlanders and sold them. The village women bought them and hid them. We had a great time. We drank every franc of the money.

We were drunk for three days. I often think of those kilts and wonder if there are any of them still there. Beautiful material, I'll swear those women never saw the like.'

'Malta,' said my cousin, 'was a foul place. They sent me there when I was wounded. It was all white and glistening, so white that it seared the eyeballs. There was a nurse there, a Welsh girl. They are a lawless race, the Welsh. God, there are times when I hate women.'

'We were passing along a road between fields one day and there were three women working there. Marvellous people, the French, the way they planted, sowed and reaped as near the fighting line as they could go, right through the war. The women stood up to watch us pass. Then one of them, a shocking old harridan, picked up her skirts and threw them over her head. The whole company broke ranks and rushed across the field. There was nothing to be done. It was a strange sight. In ordinary times not one would have touched those women, they were so old and ugly. I did not go. I was still afraid of women.'

'We went in at one door,' Justin's voice was low and monotonous. 'We paid our money and went out by another. I watched her push the money under the mattress. It made quite a lump.'

'God, weren't they awful!'

'Stout women!'

'They had to be.'

'I sometimes dream of them.'

They laughed. The light caught the white glitter of their teeth, their shining eyes.

'It's a queer thing,' said Egan. 'But all the time I was in the army I wanted to get out. I hated the lice, I loathed the rats, the mud, the food. I grumbled all day about everything. We all grumbled and cursed. But the day I got my discharge, I stood on the pavement and looked around me and I was terrified. I felt like a child who has lost his mother.'

'It wasn't so bad. We ate and drank and slept and didn't care about the morrow. If it was coming to us, it came.'

Justin's long thin fingers held the glass as if he would crush it. The fine lines of his face, almost mask-like, were thrown into relief by the lamplight. His thin, wide mouth, drawn down at one corner, trembled slightly as he spoke. His eyes were dark and pain-stricken. Egan's face was flushed and his eyes glittered, the whites slightly bloodshot. His forehead twitched as it always did when he was drunk or excited. And on his face, too, there was the same look of pain.

'They did something to us, those years, they changed us,' he said.

'They taught us the value of life and death.'

As I watched my husband and my cousin, I realized for the first time, that though they had all their limbs intact, though the only sign of war on Egan's body was a scar on the leg and here and there blue marks, each was as badly mutilated as if he had lost an arm or leg. What they had lost was more because one could not see it. The scars of war lay on their souls, and old wounds ache. A leg or arm cut off still feels. I listened as they continued their meandering conversation. When they laughed, I shuddered, for those things which excited laughter in their minds filled me with horror. God forgive me, I was frightened.

'There was a fellow in my company, a Scotchman,' said Egan, laughing. 'He wanted to get home. He was afraid to give himself a blighty so he used to sit on the cold ground every day in the hope of getting piles. "If I only had my kilt", he'd say, "it would be so much easier".'

'Ever seen a man give himself a blighty?' asked Justin. 'I never did.'

'I did. He got the main artery and was dead in ten minutes.'

'Dead men, how strange they look,' said Justin.

'I never got accustomed to looking at them. I always turned away as one does if one inadvertently comes on a man making love. One feels it an intrusion.'

'After a while I did not care so much. If I had gone on caring, I might have gone mad.'

Justin leaned forward in his chair. From beneath the heavy shock of black hair, his dark eyes glittered as if they had more facets than the eyes of man should have. He spoke slowly, his tongue thick with drink.

'I wonder if it would be the same to look at a dead woman? Have you ever looked on a dead woman? Tell me, what was it like?'

In bewilderment Egan looked from my cousin to me. Then, his face ablaze with fury, he jumped up and as he did so knocked the stool on which he had been sitting over the sleeping monkey. Before he could move, Gringo had caught his leg and bitten it. The resentment which Egan had suddenly felt towards Justin and myself was now turned on the monkey and he seized it by the throat to throttle it. Justin turned round and lifting the old clock that stood beside me on the table, hurled it at Egan. It hit him on the forehead. He staggered forward and fell on the floor, unconscious, blood streaming from his head.

I jumped out of bed and rushed over to him. Justin stood over me as I lifted Egan's head on to my lap. I could hear his heavy breathing. Beyond on the hearthrug, the little monkey jumped up and down on his hind-legs, chattering and rubbing his puny little hands. I turned to my cousin.

'You have killed him,' I cried.

'I am not sorry,' he said with bitterness.

'Go and call Bella.'

He left the room, taking Gringo with him. In a few seconds Bella arrived. In her stiff white night-gown she looked taller and stronger than ever, a tower to lean on.

'It's all right, my lamb,' she said, stroking my

shoulder. 'Here, let me have a look at him.' She laid Egan's head on the floor again, opened his shirt and laid her hand on his breast. 'It's more the drink than the blow, alanna. He'll be as right as rain in the morning. Stand back and I'll get him to bed.'

She lifted him in her strong arms and laid him on the bed, stripped him and wrapped him in the blankets. She placed a jug of water and a glass beside him. I stood by, helpless.

'Hadn't we better send for a doctor?' I asked.

'No, no, child. He'll be better in the morning. Now do you get to bed. Come, I'll tuck you up in my own. It's good and warm. He's more drunk than hurt. God in His mercy looks after drunkards and fools.'

'Can't I stay with him?'

'I'll look after him. He'll be all right, never you fear.'

She put me to bed and insisted that I should drink some whisky and milk. She sat by me and watched until I fell asleep. I did not realize that I had slept until I woke in the morning.

I awoke slowly, unwilling to come back to life. For a while I lay between waking and sleeping, the blankets drawn over my ears, my eyes tightly closed. I breathed heavily and slowly as if by doing so I might sink back again into unconsciousness. But sleep had gone and an almost intolerable pain racked me, as if I had been beaten. The day had come again and with it pain and struggle. Then across my mind flashed the picture of Gringo jumping up and down on the hearthrug, of Justin standing beside me and Egan lying bleeding on the floor. I threw back the blankets and sat up. Bella was standing beside me.

'Lie down, child,' she said.

'Egan?' I asked.

'Not a ha'porth the matter with him.'

'I must go along and see.'

She put out her hand and gently pushed me back.

'No, my lamb, you're better lying where you are. I'll bring you tea. He's been up and about this while back.'

'Where is he now?'

'He went out. He'll likely be back soon.'

I looked at her sharply. There was grief and pity in her eyes, yes, and triumph, too.

'You're lying, Bella,' I cried. 'He's gone.'

I jumped out of bed and pushed her aside. I rushed round the house in a frantic, distraught way, opening cupboards and pulling out drawers as if I had become completely demented. In and out of the rooms I rushed, searching wildly. He had gone, my love had gone, and I was left.

I found the door of Justin's room locked. I rattled the door-handle and pounded on the panels with both fists.

'Justin,' I shouted. 'Justin! Where is Egan? Tell me, where is he?'

But there came no answer. I continued shouting and banging. Then leaning against the door, I burst into tears. Bella took me by the arm and led me away.

'Don't fret, my lamb, he can't have gone far. I'll send up home for him. He'll likely be there. Come back to your bed, alanna.'

'He is gone,' I sobbed. 'Gone without a word of love, a word of farewell.'

'He's not gone far,' Bella repeated.

In spite of her insistence I would not go back to bed. I dressed hurriedly and left the house.

Egan's mother was bending over the fire when I entered the kitchen. There was no one with her. The men had all gone out to the fields. She straightened her back and turned towards me.

'Daughter,' she cried. 'What ails ye?'

'Where is Egan?'

She must have seen that it was useless to lie to me, yet she could not bring herself to answer directly.

'He'll maybe be back soon. Sit down by the fire. The kettle is on the boil and I'll make ye some tea.'

I caught her hands.

'Did he come to say good-bye?'

She looked at me, her old face calm, yet pitying.

'He did. I thought ye'd be going wi' him. But be easy, daughter, he'll send for ye.'

I could see that she had little ·faith in her own words and was merely striving to comfort me as one comforts an unhappy child with vain words and promises. She stroked my hand gently and then, standing beside me, drew my head against her side.

'When a woman bears a daughter, she should cry,' she said softly. 'Not for herself but for the pain she knows must come to her child. It is a grievous thing to be born a woman.'

I pushed her hands away. Dry sobs which I could not control tore at my throat. I had lived now for a long time with the knowledge that this would happen, yet now that it had happened, my despair was as great as if I had never known.

'Be easy, daughter,' said the old woman. 'Time takes the edge off all grief. God will take care of him and bring him safe back to us.'

Then I saw that her thought was not for me but for her son whom she feared would be lost without me.

I left her. Unconsciously I followed the old paths of my childhood. Along the road, through the fields, towards the old mill I hurried. There it stood, empty, grey and silent, a nesting-place for birds. The water flowed along the race beside the wheel, making a laughing, pleasant noise, but the wheel was still, its wooden slats worn and broken. Grass grew in the crevices of the wall and water hens nested in the bank. All around was the smell of musty corn. I leaned against the bank of the mill-race and watched the water as it flowed rapidly along and fell down again over the little weir into the river, and as it flowed it seemed to take with it some of the turmoil of my spirit. Grief gave way to anger.

I went home slowly, following the path that led through Paradise. I had not been here once since my return. I stood on the rickety little bridge that spanned the river and listened to the melancholy cawing and scolding of the crows overhead. Suddenly there came to my mind the day on which Justin had landed a trout and then, pale with fury, had dragged the hook from its jaw and hurled it back into the stream. Why had he changed from that gentle, sensitive boy? The war? Perhaps. But had he changed? — I thought. Had he not always had this bitter enmity towards his fellows, this desire to hurt them? I remembered the marble playing, and the rock he had sent hurtling down on Egan. I remembered a hundred small things. Even Nell, so happy in herself, had called him awkward. Only my early association with him had prevented me from seeing him as he really was. But now, when he had robbed me of that that I held dear, now I really understood him. I loathed him as one can only loathe one's own blood.

Beyond the bridge I saw the figure of a woman, a ragged beggar woman, seated on the bank of the river, dangling her bare toes in the water. Her unkempt grey hair fell down in straggling locks from under a tattered black hat. A black knitted shawl was tightly wound round her body and knotted at the back. As I came towards her, she raised her face and looked at me with large brown eyes.

'Theresa!' I cried.

She stretched out her hand. Could Theresa be so old? They say the mad do not age.

'A penny. Give the poor woman a penny, for the love of God and his blessed saints.'

'Don't you know me?' I asked coming closer. I could smell age, poverty, hunger from the foul rags. 'I am Loulie. Don't you remember little Loulie?'

She shook her head.

'Just one penny, kind lady, for a poor woman travelling the roads. To buy tea. A penny for the love of God.'

I took her hand in mine. The claw-like fingers closed for a moment. Then she drew her hand away and held it out again.

'Listen, Theresa, I have no pennies, not here. Over there, at the big house, there's a man called Justin. He has pennies, hundreds of them. Go and ask him. He will give you all you want. He has a kind heart for the poor.'

I turned from her and passed through the gate into the garden.

Justin was in the dining-room, seated by the fire, gazing into the coals. He did not look up when I entered the room. His eyes caught the red gleam of the fire and his long thin hands, held out to the blaze, twitched nervously. The lock of black hair fell over his forehead, giving him again that look of boyhood.

I walked up and down the room, looking at him all the while. Yet he did not move, he did not speak, he did not lift his eyes towards me. My anger was so great that the blood hammered in my temples, that it choked me. My tongue felt dry in my mouth. One thought only occupied my mind, to make him understand, to make him feel how horrible his nature was.

Then all at once my silence fell from me and I spoke. I was utterly astonished at the sound of my own voice. It came harsh and strong from my mouth. The words I spoke came from me as if another spoke them. I was by nature silent. Now the words tumbled over one another as they left my lips. Even the burden of my cry was not what I had expected. I did not speak of Egan nor of what had just happened. I went back over the years. All the accumulated anger of childhood gathered force within me. It seemed to me that I had always borne my cousin a grudge. He was what he had always been, selfish and ruthless. Why must I always walk behind him, follow in his steps, obey his command? Why did he think that he could turn towards me and away from me at will, always expecting the same obedience when it pleased him to call for it? Who made him lord and ruler over me?

I stopped for breath. Justin raised his head and looked at me.

'Why do you not answer?' I cried.

'What can I say? You are right. That is what I do expect, that you should be there when I call.'

'Why should you assume this right over me? I give my loyalty and my love where I wish and not where you wish.'

'You came back to me. I know now that no matter how often you turn away from me, you will always come back. In the end there will only be the two of us, you and I. No outsider can really touch us. You can no more escape from me than from your own shadow.'

'It is not true, Justin. I did not come back. Why should I?'

He got up and stood facing me.

'You came back, little cousin, because we love one another.'

I could hear myself laugh though I did not feel myself laugh.

'It is a lie.'

'It is no lie. Perhaps you do not know what I mean. I know that you are in love with your husband. I know that I have loved other women. But such love cannot endure. It has no roots. The love we have for one another must endure; it is of our bones and our blood. We might as well fight against the rising of the sun as fight against it. We were one flesh from the beginning.'

'You are wicked,' I cried. 'Or you are mad.'

'I may be both, but that changes nothing. I know

273

you well enough to know that had I been the first to possess you, if I had taken you that night long ago when we were together, you would not have gone to any other man. And in reality I did, Loulie. For the desire is as real as the deed.'

'How can such a thing be true? You are imagining it. You were in love with someone else. First Nell, then other women.'

'Love, love. You are confused, Loulie. What I felt was not love. They were unfortunate, unhappy, muddled creatures, and I felt sorry for them. Oh, yes, I can feel pity, though you seem to think me incapable of any feeling. But it is horrible to pity people, it is degrading. You I have never pitied, not even now when you are suffering.'

'I would hate you to pity me. I would want to kill you.'

'Because you love me.'

'No, no.'

'Answer me one question, Loulie, and answer it truthfully. As God is above I'll know if you lie. You remember that night when we lay together? Well, think back. If I had taken you then, tell me, would you have resisted? Tell me the truth, for if it should be that I am wrong, then there is no justification for me.'

'I was a child,' I pleaded.

'You were a woman.'

I looked at him, at the tall bulk of his body as he stood looking down on me and I felt weak and helpless. I wanted to shout the lie in his teeth and I could not. His dark eyes looked into mine and saw all that I would hide even from myself. I was silent.

'I knew, my dear,' he said. 'So you see why you cannot go.'

But I would not yield. My obstinacy had grown through the years of struggle. I waited for a moment before I replied.

'Justin, listen to me.' My voice was hard and insistent in my own ears. 'I love only one man now and that is not you, but Egan. If you have indeed driven him from me, then I care for no one, for there will not be left any heart in me to love. For what you have done, I hate you and will hate you until I lie in my grave.'

'Be honest. I did not drive him away. He had gone and you knew it. A week, a month, a year of suffering, that is all you would have had. I have saved you that, at least.'

'I have not asked you to save me anything.'

I turned away. He did not approach me, did not take my hand. Now that I had said what I had come to say, I felt empty of all anger and bitterness, I felt intolerably lonely. I left the room without another word, left the house and taking the car, drove away.

I TRAVELLED south to Derry, from Derry to Enniskillen, from Enniskillen to Sligo, from Sligo to Galway, then east to Dublin. From dawn to dark I drove along the roads, looking neither to left nor right. To every race-meeting in the country I went, persuaded that sooner or later Egan would turn up at one of them. It was unlikely that he would have gone back to England without money. All we had lay in my account. He could not go abroad because I carried his passport in my bag.

I searched every betting-shop in Dublin. None of the regular punters who hang around these places had seen him. I was careful how I asked for they were wary of supplying information. I always inferred that I had a tip I wished to pass on to him. It was useless. Either he had not been there or he had warned them. I did not lose heart, sure that in the end I would run him to earth.

On my way to the Fairyhouse races, the back axle of the car broke. I stood in the road and cursed it as if it were a living, sentient being. I would have to wait now until the Baldoyle meeting.

I had taken to betting in a small way. Otherwise I would have felt out of place on the race-course. It also gave me an excuse to talk to people. At Baldoyle I ran into Mary Jeffreys. She was standing on the first step of the stand, straining to see over the heads of the crowd. Beside her stood a small dark man, as precise and dapper as a cat, whom I had frequently seen at other race-meetings. I do not know why he came to the course for he never saw a race. He might as well have put on his bets over the phone in the comfort of his own house. His procedure was always the same. He would rush from one bookmaker to another to see where he could get the best price, but since he always backed the favourite, no matter what the odds, the price varied very slightly. Then he would return to his place on the first step of the stand, fix his glasses on the board and wait for the numbers to go up. This was what he was doing when I saw him with Mary Jeffreys. She was gesticulating fiercely and talking wildly. The murmur of voices rose around me as the horses approached the straight. Beside me a man kept shouting:

'Come on, Morning Sun, come on, my beauty. He's walking it, I tell ye, he's walking it. Morning Sun is walking it. Canty hasn't even got his whip up. He's walking it, it's his race.'

Silence fell on the crowd for a moment when the horses entered the straight. All one could hear was the drumming of the hooves on the turf. This is the moment for which all race-goers live, the moment when life becomes so concentrated that one cannot breathe. Then a wild shout as Beary drew his mount out of the mass of straining horse-flesh and pushed its nose past the post. Then silence again, and the cry of the bookmakers:

'Paying out on Golden Boy. Paying out on Golden Boy. Paying out . . .'

The man beside me tore up his ticket into small pieces and dropped them one by one through a crack in the step. The crowd moved restlessly about, waiting for the odds to be called for the next race and discussing the last race in a disillusioned way. I came up to Mary Jeffreys.

'Well, if it isn't the child!' she cried. 'I haven't seen you in years. Where on earth have you been? Do you know Geoff? This is Captain Geoffrey Waters, Mrs. O'Doherty.'

The little man shook hands with me, then excused himself and hurried away.

'Retired to my country estate, Mary. How's the work?'

'The paper? Oh, just the same. They come and they go, but Moriarty and I go on for ever. But I haven't been doing so well on the turf lately. Joe Canty let me down badly on this last race.'

'He couldn't have known you had your shirt on him, Mary.'

'God bless you, child, what I need is a shirt factory, working overtime. I'm going to take my friends' advice and quit this racket. Had you much on?'

'A pound on Golden Boy. I've just collected five.'

'Why in the name of God didn't I meet you before the race and not after? Where's that husband of yours?'

'Haven't you seen him? He should be somewhere about.'

'Saw him at Fairyhouse. Told me to back Morny Wing's mount. It let me down, so I suppose he's afraid to show his face. I don't bear him any grudge. There's nothing you get so much bad advice about as race-horses. Why weren't you there?'

So I had missed him at Fairyhouse.

'I couldn't get. I had a cold. How did you think he was doing? He never tells me.'

'He looked a bit down in the mouth. What have you got for the next race?'

'Strong Toddy is fancied. But don't put too much on.' I didn't know if the horse was worth a penny bet. Still, it had four legs and could run.

'I've heard it mentioned,' said Mary Jeffreys and hurried away.

Ten minutes later she was back, her soul tormented with doubt. She had just met someone else who had given her another horse.

'Tell me, Mary,' I asked. 'Did Egan say anything about Punchestown?'

'No, but he said he'd be at Leopardstown on the tenth.'

Captain Geoff Waters returned and raised his glasses.

'What did you back?' asked Mary.

'There's only one horse in this race,' he replied. 'And it's buying money, I tell you, buying money.'

'They're off!' someone shouted. Mary Jeffreys

forgot all about me. Strong Toddy won. Mary almost embraced me.

'How much had you on?' she asked.

'Nothing. I've finished for the day. I'll be moving off now. I'll be seeing you at Leopardstown.'

Egan was there on the tenth. I did not arrive until after the third race and I watched him until the fifth. He was betting carefully. He looked weary and surly as he did when he was losing. I came over and touched his arm.

'I've got the car outside, Egan, if you'd like me to drive you home.'

Without a word he left the race-course with me.

'Where?' I asked as we passed Donnybrook.

He gave the address in a low, indifferent voice, a street on the north side, off Mountjoy Square. All the way there he sat beside me, silent and forbidding, the corners of his mouth drawn tightly in.

He was living in a large bare room, formerly the drawing-room of an old Georgian house. It was horribly grimy and sordid. Everything that one touched dirtied one's hands. A chest of drawers, a table, a chair, a bed, a ragged carpet on the floor, torn curtains over dirty windows, my eye fell on one offending object after another. The bed, which had a circular canopy hung with filthy, red rep curtains, had not been made. The ashes of a dead fire lay in the grate and the hearth was covered with the ends of cigarettes.

'Take a seat,' said Egan, offering me the chair. He sat down on the bed.

'Well?' he asked. He looked at me with cold ferocity.

'Egan, why did you leave?'

'Don't waste your time and mine asking stupid questions. Do you think I could have stayed?'

'But to leave as you did without a word of explanation.'

'Explanation! What in God's name was there to explain?'

'Am I not your wife? Could you not at least have said that you were going? What have I done that you should treat me like this? Leave me without a word?'

I knew that I was saying the wrong thing. I knew that the only way to get Egan back was to ignore the whole matter and stay. My strength had always lain in my silence. Why must I talk now? Why did I say these foolish things? Yet I felt that I must.

'I have done nothing all my life but love you.'

Egan's forehead twitched and his eyes were cold with anger.

'Love me?' he almost shouted. 'You seem to think that loving me gives you some right over me. You stifle me with your love. It is with me day and night, wrapping me round like a blanket so that I cannot breathe, eating me alive. I do not want it. Do you hear? I do not want it. If you love me, let me be.'

'Egan, after all you have said, after all we have been to one another, can you turn from me now?'

'The one quality I thought you had was pride. I know you to be greedy and possessive, but I imagined you were proud. Perhaps you were only stupid. Snap out of it. It's all over. If you want a divorce, I'll see you get it.'

'Don't turn from me for what Justin has done.'

'Don't blame your cousin. In some ways you are very like him. In the same circumstances you would have acted as he did. It was through knowing him that I came to know you. Do you think I care so much about what he did? I don't. I don't care any longer about anyone, that's all. I want to go my own way alone. I want peace.'

I became angry. Why should he treat me with such brutality?

'Peace!' I cried. 'Peace! You'll never find peace. You would not want it if you could get it.'

At the sight of my anger, he was no longer angry. He came over and taking my hand made me sit down on the bed beside him.

'Lou, dear little Lou, don't force me into a position of self-defence. It makes me say cruel things which you may remember in bitterness. It's all over now. I'm sorry, too. But I never deceived you. You always knew what I was like. You took a chance and you've lost. That's all.'

'I did not ask you to marry me. You could have gone away in the beginning.'

'True. What can I say but that I'm sorry. To the day I die I shall remember all your sweet ways, all your goodness. But for the love of God, don't cling to me. I cannot bear it.'

I knew that all was lost. I had known it from the beginning. There was nothing to be done now but to accept defeat. I opened my handbag, took out his passport and some money and laid them on the table.

'I don't need the money,' he said.

'I have plenty. Take it, it is yours.'

He did not kiss me. He shook my hand as if I were a friend he had met by chance.

'Good-bye, Lou, and God have mercy on us both.'

Then, looking towards the bed, he remarked:

'Fine piece of architecture, that. The landlady says it's a bishop's bed. Fine, isn't it, to sleep at night in a bishop's bed.'

I pushed him back when he came to see me out. Slowly I walked down the stairs, through the hall. Slowly I opened the heavy hall door. I waited for a moment before I banged it behind me. But he did not call me back.

I STOOD looking up and down the street, for a moment lost. A street of ragged grandeur, wide, with high houses, broken railings, dirty windows hung with dirty curtains. From the basement the fetid smell of poverty rose, sour and nauseous. The weather was sultry and the pavement hot and dusty under foot. A corporation water van moved slowly up the street. A group of small boys who had been playing at the corner shouted and ran after it dabbling their bare feet in the sprinkling water. At the end of the street, outlined against the sky, rose the Dublin Hills, blue and distant, wavering in the heat haze. I got into the car and turned north.

Then suddenly I felt free — free as if the heavy mantel of grief had dropped from me. The tyranny of my love for Egan was past. No longer need I dread his going, no longer fear his moods, no longer suffer from the daily knowledge of his unfaithfulness. Never again would I lie awake, waiting. Never again need I feel the agony of watching my love drift from me like driftwood on the tide. That moments would come when I would again sicken was certain, but I knew that these moments would pass and my heart be light again.

The mind, released from strain, is like a kaleidoscope. Shake the barrel, look, and a pattern is formed.

285

Shake again and another comes, complete, symmetrical and entirely different. Yet all these patterns, unconnected though they seem, are similar in kind.

Justin, Egan, Tom Hennessy, they chased one another through my mind like rabbits in and out of a burrow; Justin, a small boy in long sailor trousers and a light blue linen shirt, standing high on a mound of turf sods and shouting: 'I am king of the castle'; Egan crying out: 'Peace, what I want is peace'; Tom Hennessy grinning at me and saying: 'Snap out of it, you silly girl. There's work to be done and other people to love. A man in a burning house forgets about his toothache.' I made plans for the future. I would sell the old house. Perhaps when I had finished with it, I would have rid myself of all the shadows that lay in it. I would not keep anything, not even the French clock that I loved so much. I would take Bella with me to Dublin, find a job and begin life again.

I spent the night at a small hotel in a town the name of which I did not even trouble to find out. Early the next morning I set out again. It was late when I came to Derry and the town was dark and silent. I drove straight through. In the small hours I reached home and drove the car into the cobbled yard.

I switched off the engine and sat for a while looking at the low, dark bulk of the old house outlined against the light sky of the summer night.

It rose before me, shuttered and dark. With one bright eye it leered at me and seemed to say: I am the womb to which you would return. The light from Justin's open window fell on the roof of the barn, picking out the moss-edged slates. The heavy smell of syringa, mingled with the smell of the roses, drifted over the wall from the garden, making the still air even more oppressive. It was silent as in a well. No sound from the restless sea reached my ears.

I laughed. I looked up at Justin's window and laughed. The sound was caught by the four corners of the yard and thrown back at me. So Justin was as patient or as obstinate as I was. Strange, I had not thought, even for a moment, that he might have gone. Would I let the old house fall under the auctioneer's hammer? I knew that if I did he might not be able to buy it in. Four hundred acres of land went with the house, four hundred acres in a land hungry valley. What would he say, how would he look, if I told him that I intended to force a sale? Would he be angry or would he laugh at me? Did I mean anything to Justin or was I just a part of this house and so a part of his life?

There was no need to rouse Bella. I found the back door unbolted and crept quietly into the house. My candle stood on the hall table where it had always been. For the first time I had come home and no one stood on the threshold to welcome me. Yet I felt welcome. The house itself gathered me close to it, a warm, safe place. I no longer felt afraid. Now that I had lost a great fear, the little fears fell from me. I felt enclosed and safe as a child in its mother's arms. This house did not belong to me but I to it. I yielded as a woman yields to her lover, knowing at the same time that she is the victor. This house was as much a part of me as the dead men and women whose portraits hung on the wall, as much a part of me as my cousin. I knew that I would never have sold it. It was not mine to sell.

I picked up the candle and went upstairs, no longer listening to the creaking of old wood under my feet. All was so quiet and still. In all the world only my cousin Justin and I were awake.

I stopped outside his door. I heard him move. Should I say good-night? I waited. Then the key turned in the lock. Why did he lock his door in this friendly place where no one locked doors? He stood before me, spare and tall, towering over me. The flickering light of the candle fell on his tousled hair, on his lean, dark face, freckled again by the summer sun. He was laughing.

'I have come home,' I said.

He held out his hand.

'Come along by,' he answered.